MURDER ON THE GHAN

A murder-mystery novella

GABRIEL FARAGO

This book is brought to you by Bear & King Publishing.

Publishing & Marketing Consultant: Lama Jabr
Website: https://xanapublishingandmarketing.com/
Sydney, Australia

First published 2023 © Gabriel Farago

Also by Gabriel Farago

Dear reader,

Before you start reading, just a few words about the novella as a literary genre:

The novella made its first appearance in the early Renaissance, especially in Italy and France. Giovanni Boccaccio's *The Decameron* (1349), and *Heptaméron* (1558–1559), penned by French queen Marguerite de Navarre and modelled on *The Decameron*, were the trailblazers. However, it wasn't until the late eighteenth and early nineteenth centuries that the novella took shape as the literary genre we know today.

Robert Silverberg in *Sailing to Byzantium* (2000) describes the novella as *'one of the richest and most rewarding of literary forms ... it allows for more extended development of theme and character than does the short story, without making the elaborate structural demands of the full-length book. Thus it provides an intense, detailed exploration of its subject, providing to some degree both the concentrated focus of the short story and the broad scope of the novel.'*

Murder on the Ghan is a novella and as such it is, of course, much shorter than my novels, but without losing focus or scope. That was one of the reasons I chose this genre as the vehicle to explore certain hidden corners of Jack Rogan's life, and reveal a little more about his background and character.

AUTHOR'S NOTE

Often, moments of inspiration come uninvited and in unexpected ways. This was certainly the case here. Let me tell you how it came about.

It all happened during one of the COVID-19 lockdowns in 2021, here in Australia where I live. I had just finished writing *The Death Mask Murders*, Book 7 in *The Jack Rogan Mysteries Series*, and needed some time out. Writing a book of that complexity and scope is exhausting, and after the huge amount of research involved, I was drained.

Normally, I would travel overseas after publishing a new book and attend book launches and promotions, but not so that year. Australia was a fortress: shut off from the rest of the world, which made overseas travel impossible. However, what was possible at the time, was some limited travel *within* Australia. This allowed me to embark on something I had planned for years: a trip on the legendary *Ghan*, an iconic, three-thousand-kilometre train journey through the Australian Outback.

I can still remember that moment of inspiration very clearly. It was just after sunrise. I was sitting by the window in my compartment on *The Ghan*, listening to music. There's something magical about watching the desert landscape melt out of the darkness, changing from delicate hues of mauve to pinkish-gold, and then to shades of red as the sun's first rays illuminate the barren, ancient plains dotted with mulga, and crumbling rock formations used as markers by Aboriginal tribes traversing this parched land since time immemorial.

The piece of music I was listening to was 'Lascia ch'io pianga' from Handel's opera *Rinaldo*, performed by famous Norwegian boy soprano Aksel Rykkvin. Something about Rykkvin's heavenly voice was not only very moving, but it was also inspirational.

At times, the power of music can be astounding. It can conjure up emotions and ideas in ways that are difficult to articulate and explain. As the stunning desert landscape was silently gliding past, the idea for a novella took shape. I remember reaching for my little notebook I always carry with me, and jotting down the outline of a story, with familiar characters who seemed to be sitting right next to me by the window, telling me about an extraordinary adventure that had to be told. The pages that follow are the result of that inspirational morning of literary discovery.

That said, the purpose of this novella – my fourth – is actually much broader than that. While all my books stand alone and can be read as such, readers who are familiar with all or some of the books in the series will recognise nuances and connections referring to previous storylines and characters, which will enhance the reading experience.

One character in particular, Benjamin Krakowski, stands out here because he provides a link between *Murder on The Ghan* and the very first book in the series, *The Empress Holds the Key*, while at the same time introducing a new, central character, Sophie Ritter, featured in this novella. This is, of course, quite deliberate because all my books are interconnected, often in quite subtle ways. This connection allows me to introduce and explore additional material that wasn't feasible within the framework of the much larger and more complex novels.

* * *

To further enhance your reading experience, may I suggest you listen not only to Handel's 'Lascia ch'io pianga' mentioned above, but also to Pergolesi's *Stabat Mater*, performed by Philippe Jaroussky and Emoke Barath. You can find both works on YouTube. These wonderful pieces of music feature prominently in the novella and will, in my view, add an additional dimension to, and deeper understanding of, the storyline.

Acknowledgement of Country

A few words about an important subject featured in the novella: Aboriginal themes of both historical and cultural significance.

Great care has been taken to portray Aboriginal characters in sensitive and respectful ways. After all, I am writing about the oldest living culture on the planet! All cultural topics woven into the storyline, such as Dreamtime stories and ceremonial matters, are based on meticulous research, to ensure cultural context and historical accuracy.

As a mark of respect to the Arrernte and Antakirinja peoples, I would like to conclude with an Acknowledgement of Country:

I acknowledge the Traditional Custodians of the lands featured in this novella, the Arrernte and Antakirinja people, and pay my respects to their Elders past and present. I extend that respect to Aboriginal and Torres Strait Islander peoples who may read this novella.

Gabriel Farago
Leura, Blue Mountains
November 2023

CONTENTS

Prologue: *Kupa-piti*

It all began a hundred million years ago. The world looked very different then. At that time, a vast sea covered more than sixty per cent of Australia, and that sea began to retreat. Slowly.

As the water levels fell, exposing the land, acidity levels increased in the remaining waters and began to release silica through the weathering of sandstone. About forty metres below the surface, a decaying, serpent-shaped fossil left a small cavity behind in a place that would one day become known as Coober Pedy, referred to as *Kupa-piti* – 'white man in a hole' – by local Aboriginals. The silica-rich water seeping through the sandstone found the cavity and began to slowly deposit the silica it had collected along the way, drop by drop.

As the water evaporated, it left behind a fine silica gel, which then hardened over millions of years. It took the gel about five million years to solidify into one centimetre of opal.

This marked the beginning of a long and unique geological process that would one day produce a spectacular mineraloid we know as opal, which would dazzle the eyes with a stunning display of colour as soon as it connected with sunlight. Like a buried treasure emerging from the ancient earth to reach out to the living, it would bring the gift of joy and wonder to those fortunate enough to be in the right place at the right time.

Opals have been around since ancient times. The name 'opal' has its origin in Sanskrit, *upala*, which means 'jewel'. Later, the Greeks referred to it more accurately as *opallios*, which means 'to see a change in colour'.

Yurlunggur Mine: Thursday 19 May 2023

Unable to sleep and sweating profusely, Aboriginal youth Jimmy Bingarra tossed and turned restlessly on his bunk, deep down in an opal mine in Coober Pedy. The mine was the brainchild of Andrew Simpson and 'Auntie', both Aboriginal elders, who ran a rehabilitation centre for young offenders in Alice Springs. Named after the Rainbow Serpent, *Yurlunggur*, the mine was a modest claim that had yielded just a small amount of low-grade opals. Yet the potential benefit of the mine in human terms was considerable.

The idea behind the mine project was as simple as it was effective. To give young Aboriginal offenders a second chance after coming out of prison. To help rebuild their lives, it was seen as imperative to get them away from the Alice and temptation – especially alcohol and drugs – to prevent a relapse into old habits and bad company. Sending them off to Coober Pedy to work in an opal mine run by the centre was seen by many as the answer. And in many ways, it had worked remarkably well in reforming young offenders and integrating them back into society.

For days, Jimmy had heard a voice whispering seductively in his ear about a precious opal in the mine, just waiting to be discovered. One of Jimmy's heroes was Jandamarra, an 1890s Aboriginal freedom fighter who had refused to surrender his country and his freedom to the white settlers pushing relentlessly north. Jandamarra died at Tunnel Creek in the Kimberley, and became a legend.

Exhausted, Jimmy finally drifted into a slumber and began to dream. In the dream, Jandamarra appeared and told him about a rare, precious opal that had been waiting for aeons to be discovered in one of the abandoned mine shafts deep in the bowels of the ancient earth.

Bathed in sweat, Jimmy woke suddenly. As he focused his eyes, he could see an apparition of Jandamarra next to his bunk. He was pointing to one of the mine shafts and began to float towards it, the invitation obvious. Mesmerised, Jimmy got up, reached for his torch and tool bag, and followed Jandamarra down into the shaft. The old shaft had been abandoned decades earlier due to a poor yield. At the end of the shaft, Jandamarra stopped, pointed to a ridge just below the low ceiling and whispered *'Yurlunggur'*, before his image floated away.

Jimmy put down his tool bag, pulled out his hammer and chisel, and began to dig into the stone. He didn't have to dig for long. Only centimetres below the surface, Jimmy saw the rock begin to crumble and change colour. He recognised the signs immediately. This was no longer sandstone, but something quite different: a rare, priceless opal!

His heart beating like a drum, it took Jimmy only a few minutes to dig out the serpent-shaped opal, the largest and most stunning he had ever seen. Holding the heavy piece up against the torchlight, Jimmy whispered *'Yurlunggur'*, just as Jandamarra had done moments earlier, and let his fingertips glide over the smooth, sparkling surface, his eyes wide with astonishment and wonder as the full implications of the extraordinary find began to sink in.

What Jimmy hadn't noticed in his excitement was that he was being watched. Toby Doongur, a rebellious and violent Aboriginal youth working at the mine under Jimmy's direction as part of his parole conditions, had heard the digging noise deep down in one of the shafts, and had followed the sound to investigate.

Sydney Opera House: Saturday 21 May

A hush of anticipation descended on the great Concert Hall of Sydney Opera House, signalling the imminent entry of Sophie Ritter, the much-anticipated guest conductor. As soon as the side doors opened, thunderous applause erupted as Ritter walked confidently towards the waiting orchestra, shook hands with the First Violin, and then turned to face the audience.

A female conductor in the male-dominated world of music was rare, but Ritter was an exceptional talent impossible to ignore. Her talent, which sparkled like a precious gem, had opened some of the forbidding doors guarded by antiquated traditions that had kept women firmly on the outside for centuries.

A youthful-looking, vivacious woman in her forties, she was dressed in a black designer trouser suit and shirt, with a white silk scarf elegantly draped around her neck, her only jewellery a beautiful set of pearl earrings – a gift from her parents. Ritter radiated confidence and style befitting someone at the pinnacle of her career.

Sitting directly in front of the orchestra in one of the best seats in the house, Jack Rogan turned to Jana Gonski, a former Australian Federal Police officer and close friend, sitting next to him. 'She looks so young, don't you think?'

'What did you expect? A female Bernstein with white hair?'

'Of course not, but not—'

'Someone so vibrant and attractive?'

'Aha.'

Gonski smiled. She could read Jack like a book. He obviously found Ritter very alluring and was drawn to her aura of confidence and charm.

Jack turned to Dr Rosen sitting on his other side. 'It's so wonderful you could make it. Benjamin will be thrilled.'

'I wouldn't have missed this for the world. If only you knew what strings I had to pull in Kenya to get here—'

'Not the first time, I bet,' said Marcus Carrington, who sat next to Dr Rosen. 'Benjamin will be delighted. Have you seen him yet?'

'No. Like him, I only flew in last night, and he's been in rehearsals ever since. We only spoke on the phone.'

Jack nodded. 'I've arranged supper in my apartment after the concert, which as you know is only a short walk from here. We can all catch up then.'

'No doubt about you, Jack, you always find the right way,' said Jana.

'I try.'

Ritter turned towards the side door and raised her arm in a gesture of welcome as Maestro Krakowski, celebrated composer and violin virtuoso – the star attraction of the evening – walked on stage. Dressed formally in a dinner suit, with his famous violin, the Empress, tucked under his arm, Krakowski swept into the hall, walked up to Ritter, and kissed her on both cheeks. As the evening's programme informed the audience, Ritter had been 'discovered' by Krakowski as a teenager in Salzburg, and had been his protégée ever since. In many ways she owed her phenomenal success to his guiding hand, and he viewed her as the daughter he never had.

Krakowski turned to face the audience, lifted his violin to his chin and closed his eyes. This was a moment of total concentration, shutting out everything but the music welling up from somewhere deep within. For an instant, Krakowski remembered his father in Auschwitz telling him 'Don't forget, my son, the Empress holds the key'. Smiling, Krakowski opened his eyes, looked at Ritter and nodded ever so slightly. His second violin concerto was about to begin.

Dr Rosen reached for Jack's hand and held it tightly as the first notes of the concerto rose to the lofty ceiling, filling the huge concert hall with sublime sound. Moments later the violin entered, and tears began to roll down Dr Rosen's cheeks as the beauty of the music flooded her heart with joy. Feeling her hand tremble, Jack squeezed it in silent reply.

After the concert: Jack's apartment

As Jack and Dr Rosen were leaving their seats after the last of the applause had ebbed away, an usher walked up to them and asked them to accompany him backstage.

The backstage area reserved for the orchestra was chaotic. Holding a large bouquet of stunning flowers in her arms, Ritter stood by a panoramic window overlooking the harbour. Surrounded by excited musicians all trying to talk to her at once, she looked like a movie star holding court at the Oscars.

Krakowski, who stood a few paces behind her, was showing his violin, a Stradivarius, to the awe-struck violinists who were admiring the famous instrument. Presented by Count Esterhazy to Krakowski's father, a child prodigy, before a concert in Vienna in 1905, the violin, which already had a long history at the time, became an instant sensation, and made Krakowski's father a celebrity.

The reason the violin had been presented to the young virtuoso was due to an unfortunate incident that almost derailed the concert. His own violin had been stolen by gypsies the day before the performance. Having heard about the theft, the count graciously presented the distraught boy with the famous violin just before the concert started because, he said, there was no-one else in the empire who could play it like him.

As soon as Krakowski saw Dr Rosen coming towards him, he walked over to her and embraced her. 'I can't tell you what this means to me, Bettany,' he said, holding her tight. 'You came!' Krakowski and Dr Rosen went back a long way and were very close.

'A special moment, wouldn't you say?' said Gonski to Jack, who stood next to her, watching.

Jack nodded. 'Those two have been through a lot together.'

'So have we all,' said Carrington.

'True,' said Gonski. 'And so has the violin.'

Leading Ritter by the hand, Krakowski walked over to Jack and the others. 'Thank you for coming, my friends. Let me introduce you to Sophie. I think she needs rescuing, don't you agree, Jack?'

'She seems to be coping rather well. With the adulation, I mean,' replied Jack, smiling.

As soon as Jack shook hands with Ritter and looked into her eyes, something happened. It was an instant bond and fascination that had no rational explanation, but was nevertheless real and, more importantly perhaps, exciting.

'That was some concert back there,' said Jack, enjoying the closeness of the fascinating woman he had just met.

'I've heard a lot about you from Benjamin over the years,' said Ritter, sizing up Jack as she tried to reconcile the man her mentor had spoken about so often with the man standing in front of her, who somehow seemed to be drawing her into his orbit.

It was a strange, seductive feeling for a woman who had dedicated her entire life to her career. But that had come at a price. Serious relationships didn't fit into the life of a celebrity conductor touring the concert halls of the world. Loneliness in exchange for fame and success was the price she had to pay, because nothing in life is free.

'I have arranged a little supper for us in my apartment, which is very close by. You will join us, I hope?' said Jack. 'We can walk.'

Ritter gave Jack a coquettish look. 'If I'm invited ...'

'Of course you are. Supper without the star of the evening just wouldn't be the same.'

'Good. I'm starving. I barely ate anything since I arrived. And I don't eat before a concert.'

'Ah. Then let me do something about that. I'm often accused of always being hungry. At least we seem to have that in common.'

'I'm sure that's not going to be the only thing,' replied Ritter, lowering her voice. 'But before you invite this starving musician to dinner, I have a confession to make.'

'A confession? Already? How intriguing,' said Jack, raising an eyebrow in mock surprise.

'It's best to clear the air right from the beginning.'

'I agree. Sounds serious. So, what's this confession all about?'

'Despite Benjamin having spoken about you in glowing terms for years, I haven't read any of your books.'

'Is that it?'

'It is.'

'That's a relief.'

'*Relief?* How so?'

'I usually get the opposite news from people I meet for the first time. They seem to think they know me because they *have* read all my books. Can be very tedious and annoying.'

Ritter began to laugh. 'The price of fame, I suppose.'

'Once you're out there in the public domain, life's no longer your own, as my publicist keeps reminding me.'

'Does that bother you?'

'Not at all. I just keep doing my own thing, much to the annoyance of my exasperated publicist, who wrote me off years ago as a lost cause, but is still trying to reform me, poor love ...'

Ritter put her hand on Jack's arm, her touch making the hairs on the back of his neck tingle. 'Benjamin and I will have to talk to some of the musicians before we can leave.'

'Once out there in the public domain ...?'

'Something like that. I can see you understand.'

'Perfectly. We'll wait outside.'

'Wow! This is some apartment,' said Ritter, stepping out onto the large penthouse terrace overlooking the Opera House with the illuminated arc of the iconic Harbour Bridge behind it. 'You live here?'

'When I'm in Sydney, yes, which is unfortunately not as often as I would like. Most of the time I live in France.'

'Ah. The Kuragin chateau. Benjamin talks about that often. The dramatic rescue of Anna, Countess Kuragin's daughter.'

Jack shook his head. 'Looks like my entire life's an open book here.'

'Don't worry, only among friends. That painting you showed me earlier is amazing.'

'Yes, Anna painted it. She's very talented. That's how she remembered her rescue in that cave in Outback Australia. It was a very moving present.'

'Ah, there you are,' said Gonski. 'I've been looking for you. Two waiters are at the door carrying huge platters—'

'That would be our supper; excellent. Please excuse me,' said Jack.

Gonski linked arms with Ritter and together they admired the stunning view of Circular Quay with the city skyline behind it, and across to a huge ocean liner tied up at the Overseas Passenger Terminal in front of The Rocks.

'This is magical,' said Ritter.

'Your first time in Sydney?'

'Yes. My first time in Australia.'

'Your performance was amazing,' said Gonski. 'What an extraordinary life you must lead.'

'In many ways it is,' replied Ritter, a tinge of sadness in her voice. 'And it's all due to Benjamin. He's the real talent here, you know. He composed that violin concerto and performed it. He can play the violin like no other. He's a true virtuoso and an extraordinary conductor as well; a genius. He connects with music like no-one else I've ever come across.'

'And you are his protégée?'

'I suppose I am that. I owe him everything.'

'He must see something very special in you ...'

'All right, you two,' said Jack, waving from the open terrace door. 'You better come inside. Supper's served.'

After a superb seafood meal and copious quantities of excellent New Zealand wines, including a sauvignon blanc and one of Jack's favourites, a pinot noir from Central Otago, the atmosphere in the apartment became intimate and the conversation animated, as is only possible among a group of friends who know each other well.

'You are a fortunate guy, Jack,' said Ritter. 'You have wonderful friends.'

'I know. And this is a very rare and special evening. For all of us. We don't often have an opportunity to get together like this. Take Marcus over there, for instance,' said Jack, pointing to Carrington talking to Krakowski. 'He lost his wife and daughter in a terrorist attack in Egypt. During a spectacular concert at the Karnak temple, would you believe: *Aida*. Jana was there and witnessed it all.'

'Benjamin told me about that and how you found his violin.'

'The first time I met Benjamin was during a masterclass he was giving in London. Jana and I were following the trail of a Nazi war criminal.'

'And that trail led you to Benjamin's violin. I know the story. Benjamin told it to me many times. He also speaks a lot about Doctor Rosen.'

'They have a special bond, but their lives keep them apart. Benjamin tours the concert halls of the world, and Bettany works tirelessly in Third World countries, looking after the underprivileged and destitute.'

'Amazing.'

'All right, you two. I can see you are getting along just fine,' said Krakowski as he walked up to Ritter and Jack sitting by the open doors. 'It's after midnight; I think it's time to go.'

'That late already?' said Ritter, about to stand up.

Jack put a hand on hers. 'There's no need to rush. Your hotel's just over there. A ten-minute walk. I'll walk you home later, if you like ...'

Ritter looked at Jack. He was the most exciting man she had met in years, and he was sending her a signal. She realised this was another fork in the road of a busy life dominated by regimented commitments.

For an instant, Ritter locked eyes with Jack and what she saw made her heart beat faster. Decision time. She could take up Jack's offer and stay, or stand up and leave with the others.

'I would like that, thank you,' she said, surprising herself. 'It's a magical evening. I don't want it to end.'

'It doesn't have to.' Jack stood up. 'I'll say goodnight to my guests and will be right back. Don't go anywhere.'

Ritter smiled at Jack, relieved because she had found the courage to take up his offer, the thought of being alone with him making her feel slightly breathless.

A few minutes later, Jack returned with two brandy balloons and a bottle of cognac.

'Nightcap?' he said and opened the bottle.

'Why not? You are the perfect host.'

'And you are one of the most exciting women I've met in a long time.'

'I bet you say this to all of them.'

'Only the pretty ones.' Jack ran his fingers through his hair and handed Ritter her drink.

Ritter burst out laughing. The ice was broken and they had comfortably slipped into an intimacy that was rare after just a brief meeting. 'Cheers!'

Ritter lifted her glass and looked at Jack, wondering where this magical moment would take her.

The next morning: Sunday 22 May

Shielding her eyes from the sun's glare, Sophie adjusted the bathrobe she had borrowed from Jack and stepped out onto the terrace. Taking a deep breath, she let her eyes roam over the stunning eggshell-shaped roof of the Opera House, its white tiles reflecting the morning sun like hundreds of mirrors trapping the first light of the day.

It was just after sunrise, and everything looked different in the morning. Running her fingers through her short, auburn hair, Sophie smiled. To her surprise, she had absolutely no regrets about having decided to stay and let the magic of the evening take its course. On the contrary, instead of perhaps feeling a little awkward, she felt remarkably relaxed and refreshed, even after just a few hours' sleep.

Looking around, Sophie could see Jack through the open kitchen window. 'Fresh orange juice is ready, and so is the coffee,' Jack called out. 'Come and get it. I can't leave the stove.'

Barefoot and dressed in a pair of baggy shorts and a T-shirt, with an apron – bearing a picture of a smiling garlic clove – wrapped around his waist, Jack was busily working at the stove. 'Perfect timing,' he said. 'Scrambled eggs with smoked salmon and avocado coming up. Why don't you look after the toast over there? It must be almost ready. I set a table outside.'

'Domesticity is one thing I hadn't expected from you, Jack.'

'Necessity is a good teacher. I'm a bachelor, don't forget. And besides, I like cooking,' Jack prattled on and took the frying pan off the stove. 'Here we go ...'

'This is absolutely delicious, Jack,' said Sophie, munching happily. 'I haven't felt so relaxed in months.'

'Then we're off to a good start. I got up early and made some calls.'

'You did? What about?'

'Your holiday.'

'I don't understand.'

'You told me last night you had six free days before the next concert in Adelaide, and that you wanted to see some of Australia

12

during that time. You mentioned the Outback. You also mentioned adventure ...'

'Yes, but—'

'You also said you hadn't made any arrangements, and that Benjamin was planning to spend some time with Bettany in Queensland. Which means you are on your own. How am I doing so far?'

'True, but—'

'Well, I have friends in the travel business and they are putting something together as we speak. And besides, when it comes to adventure, I'm your man.'

'What do you mean?'

'It's quite simple, really. You have six days – not much considering the size of this continent – and no travel arrangements. As of now, this has changed.'

'In what way?'

'If you'll allow me to be your guide, I'd like to show you some of the iconic sights this remarkable country has to offer. I grew up in the Outback, remember, and know this place well. And besides, I was planning to spend a few days in the country in any event. More coffee?'

'If I understand you correctly, you are suggesting we tour Outback Australia *together*?'

'Exactly. We're booked on a flight to Alice Springs later this morning. You'll love Alice, and there's something special on this afternoon that I know you will enjoy. I was planning to go there anyway and have a look.'

Sophie shook her head. 'I don't know what to make of this.'

'Nothing to worry about. Just leave it all to me. All you have to do is go back to your hotel and pack. Keep it simple: shorts, sandals, T-shirts; stuff like that. It'll be hot. And then we're off to the airport. How does that sound?'

Sophie put down her cutlery, stood up and walked over to Jack. Bending down she put her arms around his neck and kissed him gently on one cheek.

Jack looked up and pointed to the other cheek. 'What about this one?'

Sophie laughed and kissed Jack passionately on the mouth.

Alice Springs: the race

During the entire three-hour flight, Sophie had had her face pressed against the window like an excited child, taking in the stunning red, yellow and ochre colours of the Outback desert landscape gliding past below looking like something out of a *National Geographic* documentary. 'I had no idea it would be this beautiful. And so different,' she said, turning to Jack sitting next to her.

'You ain't seen nothing yet, kiddo. Wait till you see all this from the ground, especially the West MacDonnells.' Jack pointed to an undulating, caterpillar-shaped mountain range in the distance. 'That's them over there. Stunning country with the oldest river in the world; the Finke River is thought to be more than three hundred million years old.'

'*Kiddo*? What's that?'

'An Aussie term of endearment. After all, we're about to land in the Outback. And where I'm about to take you, well, the lingo is going to be a little different. Better get used to it.'

'Lingo?'

'Yep. The language. You'll find that folk speak a little differently out here. Especially where we're going' – Jack looked at his watch – 'straight from the airport. We'll leave our luggage there and collect it later. If we do that, we should just make it.'

'Are you going to tell me where we are going?'

'No. It's a surprise. You wanted adventure, remember?'

'True.'

'A little different from the concert hall?'

'Sure is.'

'That was the idea. Buckle up, we're about to land.'

The first thing everyone seemed to notice on arrival at Alice Springs was the dry heat and intense glare that made lips crack and eyes water. The hot air baked the red earth, and the rugged hills in the distance shimmered like liquid glass in the midday sun as Jack and Sophie walked out of the terminal and caught a taxi.

14

The racetrack on the outskirts of Alice was just a short ride from the airport.

'Here we are,' said Jack. 'This should be quite something.'

Sophie looked at the huge crowd walking towards what looked like some kind of showground with marquees, banners advertising beer, tents, and all kinds of vehicles and trailers, converted vintage buses and ancient caravans parked along the way. Somewhere in the distance, a band was playing country and western music.

'What's this? Some kind of country fair?' said Sophie, as Jack helped her out of the taxi.

'Of sorts,' said Jack, laughing. 'We have to walk from here. Come.'

'Of sorts? What do you mean?'

'This is the inaugural Larapinta Cup. A historic event. Years of planning have gone into this. You wouldn't want to miss this for the world.'

'A race? What kind of race?'

'A unique one. You'll see why in a moment. We're almost there. I've got tickets for refreshments in that marquee over there. And in that marquee, the CWA – the Country Women's Association – is doing a wonderful job. Their cakes are legendary.'

Shaking her head, Sophie looked at Jack. 'You planned to come here all along, didn't you?'

'Aha,' said Jack, grinning sheepishly. 'I have lots of mates here. You're about to meet a few of them.'

'I see,' said Sophie, feeling a little apprehensive about being pushed along by the colourful, albeit it a little rowdy crowd making their way to the entry.

Just then, a mountain of a man dressed in torn jeans, a checked shirt and a huge, broadbrimmed hat with a crocodile-skin headband walked up to Jack from behind and slapped him on the back.

'You made it, mate,' said the man.

'*Rusty*! Wouldn't miss it for quids. You're riding?'

'Sure. I entered Rosie. She's just over there getting ready.'

'Well, that should be quite something, mate.'

'You bet! I see you brought a friend,' said Rusty, turning to Sophie watching him, his bushy red beard giving him a roguish, bushranger look.

'That's Sophie. We just flew in. She's a conductor,' said Jack, lowering his voice.

Rusty extended his huge hand. 'Please to meet you, love. You work on the trams? Melbourne? I've been to Melbourne once—'

Jack burst out laughing. 'Not that kind of conductor, mate.'

'What do you mean?'

'Never mind. Another time. You better get ready. Look, Rosie's waiting!'

'Sure thing. See you after the race. We'll have a few beers.'

'You bet.'

Sophie watched Rusty swagger away, his well-worn boots kicking up the dust, and pointed ahead, her eyes wide with astonishment. 'Is that Rosie?'

'Yes, that's her.'

'But that's a *camel*.'

'Sure. This is a camel race. Can I get you a beer?'

The first race started at three pm sharp. Rosie was a starter in the second race.

'Just stay here for a moment,' said Jack as the first race ended. 'I'm going to place a bet with the bookie over there.' Jack pointed to a man with a huge leather bag strapped around his waist, surrounded by eager punters holding up bundles of cash. Jack managed to place a bet just before the start of the race and return to Sophie standing at the barrier.

'Here we go,' said Jack. 'Rosie's the favourite. She won the Camel Cup last July here in Alice. She's a legend. And so is Rusty. Camel racing started here thirty years ago in a dry river bed: the Todd River.'

'I never knew there were camels in Australia,' said Sophie.

'Camels were introduced to South Australia by Afghan cameleers in the early eighteen hundreds, to help explore the harsh interior. Perfect transport in the Outback, which was often too difficult to traverse with horses or bullock carts, especially during a drought. Camels have been thriving here ever since. In fact, there are so many in the wild now, they pose a big problem in the national parks. Introduced species rarely mix well with local fauna and flora.'

Moments later, the tinny loudspeakers attached to the top of poles crackled into life, as the race was formally announced and seven temperamental camels lined up at the starting line.

'This is incredible,' said Sophie, her face flushed with excitement as the roar of the crowd all but drowned out the starting gun. Within seconds the camels were out of the barrier and on their way. While their running style looked awkward, their speed was astonishing. How the riders managed to stay in the saddles strapped to the back of the camels was a mystery.

Rosie got off to a good start. Rusty, now wearing a red helmet, looked formidable as he led Rosie into the first turn. This was always tricky, as camels tended to bump into one another in the turn, causing all kinds of mayhem, to the great delight of the crowd expecting something like that.

The way to avoid a collision that could easily result in a rider falling off, or worse, was to be at the front, and that was exactly where Rusty had positioned Rosie, who seemed to be enjoying herself and was moving with surprising speed towards the next turn.

That's when Rambo, Rosie's main rival, made his move. His rider had carefully positioned Rambo in the inside lane as he approached the turn. This would make overtaking Rosie possible if Rambo's stamina kept up.

Rusty could see Rambo approaching from behind and knew exactly what his rival was up to. If Rosie could just manage to put on a little extra speed, she might just foil the overtaking manoeuvre. After that, it was plain sailing down the strait to the finish line. Rusty talked to Rosie constantly and was pleased to see her respond exactly as he had hoped. Rambo was nowhere to be seen, so Rusty assumed he must be falling behind. The roar of the crowd certainly seemed to suggest that.

Now moving at top speed with the finish line in sight, Rusty sensed victory. That's when the unexpected happened.

A stray dog suddenly came out of nowhere and ran onto the track only a few metres in front of Rosie, who was closing in at full speed. Spooked by the sudden appearance of the unexpected intruder, Rosie tried instinctively to avoid running into him, and suddenly veered to the left. Unable to hold on, Rusty was thrown out of his saddle and hit the ground with a bone-crunching thump just as Rambo roared past him, the camel's hoofs barely missing his head as the rest of the field came up from behind. Rosie, by now riderless, continued to run towards the finish line and came second. Obviously, without a rider, she would be disqualified.

'*Bugger!*' said Jack and tore up the betting chits. 'So close; can you believe it? Let's hope Rusty's all right. That was quite a nasty fall for a big bloke.'

'Look, there he goes,' shouted Sophie as Rusty stood up, dusted himself off, took off his helmet, and then limped off the track towards the beer tent.

'Doesn't look like he's broken anything – this time. Nothing a couple of schooners won't fix, and there will be plenty wanting to shout him a few beers in the tent, that's for sure.' Jack turned to Sophie standing next to him. 'What did you think of the race?'

'I haven't seen anything quite like it. It's been wonderful. You promised adventure and you delivered!'

'He usually does,' said a voice from behind. Jack turned around.

'Andrew! How wonderful to see you,' said Jack, embracing an elderly Aboriginal man.

'I thought you might come. It's been quite a long time.'

'This is Sophie Ritter, a famous conductor from Vienna,' said Jack, introducing Sophie.

'Welcome to the Outback,' said Simpson.

'Andrew and I were involved in the rescue of Anna Popov,' said Jack. 'In fact, without Andrew she may never have been found.'

'What fascinating friends you have, Jack,' said Sophie, enjoying herself. 'First there was Rusty, and now Mister Simpson.'

'Fascinating is one word for it; I could think of a few more,' said Simpson, laughing. 'So, you already met Rusty. Quite a character. Nasty fall, though. He'll be drowning his sorrows in the beer tent by now, for sure.'

'Do you think we could visit your gallery, perhaps this afternoon? I would love to show Sophie your collection. That would really give her an insight into Aboriginal art and culture.'

'Sure. Come past any time. You know where I am. I better go and join the boys in the tent,' said Simpson. 'See you later.'

'What an interesting man,' said Sophie after Simpson had left.

'He certainly is. In many ways. He's a retired police officer and now runs an art gallery specialising in Indigenous art, and he helps young Aboriginal offenders find their way after jail time. His personal collection is perhaps one of the best in the Outback. Wait till you see it. Now, let's sample some scones and cakes in the CWA tent over there before they're all gone. Cakes first, beer tent later, art after that. Come.'

Alice Springs: Wandjina Gallery

After collecting a hire car and their luggage from the airport and settling into their hotel, Jack took Sophie straight to Simpson's gallery on the outskirts of Alice. The appearance of the modest house was deceptive, the simple 'Wandjina Gallery' sign above the door the only indication of the surprises waiting within.

Sophie gasped as soon as she entered. Almost at once, she was greeted by spectacular paintings of spirit beings and creation stories, delving deep into the collective memory of the longest living culture on the planet.

'What do you think?' said Jack.

'I've never seen anything quite like it. *Breathtaking!*'

Pleased by Sophie's reaction, Simpson took her on a tour, including to his private rooms in the back where he kept his own collection of pieces he couldn't bear to part with. It was there they came across a lifesize bark painting of Dinkarra, a Dreamtime hero.

Simpson turned to Jack. 'We stood right here with Cassandra, remember?' he said.

'Sure do. You asked her if she could hear anything when looking at Dinkarra.'

'And she said she could hear the whisper of generations past. A curious reply, wouldn't you say?'

'Perhaps. And then you asked her if she could understand what they were saying, right?'

'And she replied no, she couldn't understand what they were saying, but she could *feel* what they meant. That was Cassandra.'

'Who was Cassandra?' asked Sophie.

'Cassandra was a gifted Māori psychic who played an important role in Anna Popov's rescue. Tragically, she lost her life in a Broome hospital, protecting Anna from an assassin.'

Jack paused and ran his fingers through his hair, the painful memory clearly showing on his face. 'She's the mother of Tristan, one of the most remarkable young men I have ever met. He's a psychic just like his mum was, only his gift is more powerful.'

'He can hear the whisper of angels and glimpse eternity,' said Simpson. 'Just like some of these artists here who tried to capture Dreamtime concepts and traditions in their paintings, and give them visual expression.'

Sophie shook her head and turned to Jack standing next to her. 'Now I understand why Benjamin calls you—'

'What?' said Jack.

'An adventure junkie.'

'That's a good one,' said Simpson, laughing. 'That just about sums him up beautifully. Tea, anyone?'

Irresistibly drawn to some of Simpson's paintings that she found particularly moving, Sophie spent time standing silently in front of a set of striking paintings in the next room, leaving Jack and Simpson momentarily alone.

'Remarkable young woman,' said Simpson, sipping his tea.

'She is; a true artist. According to Benjamin, one of the most talented conductors of our time. And like all true artists, she sees the world through a different lens. In her case, it's all about music.'

'You seem to be getting on well.'

'We are, bearing in mind we only met a couple of days ago.'

Simpson shook his head. 'No doubt about it, Jack. You're a chick magnet.'

Jack laughed and waved dismissively.

'So, what's the plan?' asked Simpson.

'We're flying to Uluru tomorrow. I want to show her the Rock and the national park. I have a tour of Kata Tjuta planned for the afternoon; a helicopter flight. The area looks fantastic from above. Only then can you appreciate the full scale and impact of those stunning rock formations, and understand why they've been considered sacred since time immemorial. Then it's back here for one night.'

'And then what?'

'I managed to secure a cabin on *The Ghan* back to Adelaide. That's a surprise. She doesn't know. Wasn't easy, but that should be something special, don't you think?'

'Definitely. And don't forget, *The Ghan* stops at Manguri, which allows you to visit Coober Pedy; it isn't far.'

'I know. A tour's included as part of the journey. That place is about as unique and Aussie as it gets, don't you think?'

'Sure is. An underground mining village populated by colourful old-timers and eccentrics living in hope.'

'Different, for sure.'

'We run a small mining claim there, you know. As part of our rehabilitation program for young offenders.'

'Great idea. Does it work?'

'It does, but sadly not for all. By the way, thank you again for your generous donations. You haven't missed a year. Every dollar helps.'

'I admire what you and Auntie are doing there. Makes a real difference to young lives. That's what counts.'

'Glad you think so.'

Jack put down his cup and stood up. 'We must get going. It's been a long day.'

'Camel racing can be exhausting, especially the beer tent ...'

'True. It's been great to see you, Andrew.'

'And you.'

Alice Springs, the Drover's Retreat: Tuesday 24 May

'Well,' what did you think of Uluru?' said Jack, as the plane lined up for landing in Alice.

Sophie reached for Jack's hand and squeezed it. 'Breathtaking! A spiritual place. Thank you. A real adventure I won't forget.'

'Good. And there's a lot more to come …'

'What do you mean?'

'It doesn't stop there, you know. We still have a few days before you have to be in Adelaide for that concert.'

Sophie leaned across and kissed Jack on the cheek. 'You're a dark horse, Jack Rogan.'

'I've been called worse.'

'Are you going to tell me what you've planned?'

'No, except for this: tonight we're having dinner in an authentic outback pub. Best steaks in the district. The real thing, full of outback characters. Rusty will be there.'

'And a few of your other friends, I suppose?'

'Yep. They've all heard about you and want to meet you.'

'Sure.'

'They all want to meet the famous conductor who has nothing to do with trams, but is working in concert halls,' teased Jack, a sparkle in his eyes. 'Rusty spread the word. News travels fast in the Outback.'

'You're setting me up.'

'No, just a little fun. They're all great blokes. You may even meet Olive.'

'Who's Olive? Another camel?' ventured Sophie, laughing.

'You'll find out tonight.'

The first thing one noticed when approaching Alice Springs icon the Drover's Retreat was the strange vehicles parked in front of it. Because many of the regular patrons lived outside Alice and had to travel quite long distances, many of the vehicles were unique and full of character. One in particular looked like something out of *Mad Max*. A cross

23

between a tractor and tow truck, it was difficult to imagine how such a vehicle was allowed on the road in the first place. To begin with, there was no windscreen and no cabin as such. The driver sat out in the open just behind the huge engine. A ferocious-looking dog sat in the passenger seat, faithfully guarding his domain.

Jack pointed to the strange vehicle. 'Looks like Rusty's already here.'

'That's his car?'

'Well, you couldn't really call it a car. He tows Rosie's trailer with that contraption. Seems to work okay. Because Rosie doesn't fit into a horse float, he had to build something special for her.'

'Fascinating.'

'Rusty has taken the roof off a large horse float so that Rosie, who is quite tall, can have some headspace and can see where she's going. Keeps her calm, he reckons.'

'Interesting ...'

'And Rusty usually wears goggles and a vintage leather helmet like early aviators used when flying those open biplanes. To keep the dust out. Occasionally, Rosie wears goggles too. It's quite a sight, I can tell you. Tourists love it.'

'I can imagine. The Red Baron of the Outback.'

'Something like that. Come on, let's go inside. You're in for a treat.'

I was afraid of that, thought Sophie, but didn't say anything.

From the outside, the Drover's Retreat looked a bit like a Wild West saloon with a huge veranda and swinging doors. 'They've done this place up a lot since I was here last time,' said Jack, holding Sophie's hand. 'New roof. It used to be a real dump, but the beer was always cold, the steaks gigantic, and the atmosphere priceless. Let's hope nothing's changed.'

The music inside the huge, crowded room was deafening. A long bar at the back dominated. A dozen bar staff serving drinks were joking with eager patrons lined up three deep to place their orders. On one side, the room opened out onto a walled courtyard. The centrepiece of the courtyard was a massive charcoal grill where several Aboriginal

24

chefs were cooking enormous steaks, the mouthwatering aroma of sizzling meat and onions filling the air.

'What do you think?' asked Jack, navigating through the excited crowd.

'I don't quite know what to think,' said Sophie, holding on tight. 'It's different.'

'Like a setting for an outback opera, perhaps?' teased Jack.

'Not bad. Could be. We could introduce some of those Aboriginal didgeridoos you told me about.'

'A couple of visiting performers from around here would create quite a stir in Vienna, don't you think?'

'Sure. Perhaps we could persuade Rusty to come along? What do you think?' said Sophie.

'With Rosie?'

'That could be a little difficult. The Viennese audience is very conservative.'

'Hmm. There, look.' Jack pointed to a large round table in the courtyard. 'Rusty and his mates. Come, let's say hello.'

Within moments, Sophie was surrounded by eager young men trying to buy her a drink, and a group of giggling girls wearing Akubra hats, hand-stitched boots, and impossibly tight jeans, trying to impress the young men.

Jack sat down next to Rusty. 'How are you, mate?'

'Still a bit sore. Pity about the race. So bloody close.'

'Bummer! Rosie should have won!'

'Next time. Them's the breaks. Your conductor lady seems to be enjoying herself.'

'She is. It's a different world out here, especially for someone like her.'

'And for you, mate?'

'I'm at home here. I grew up in the Outback – just like you, remember?'

'You're a lucky bastard, Jack. Do you want to know why?'

'Tell me.'

'You're at home wherever you go.'

'I suppose that's true,' said Jack, a little surprised by the shrewd observation coming from a simple man who'd spent most of his life on a remote cattle station.

'Not many can do that. Beer?'

'Sure. And then a steak. I'm starving!'

After a hearty dinner washed down with copious quantities of beer, the dance floor in the courtyard came to life. The music became even louder, and so did the patrons on the dance floor.

Jack turned to Sophie sitting next to him. 'Would you like to meet Olive?'

'Who's Olive?'

Jack pointed to a tall man wearing a huge hat standing at the bar. The man was surrounded by a group of women pointing excitedly to something around his neck. 'That's my mate Buster. He's a national parks ranger. Come, I'll introduce you.'

As Jack pushed through the crowd and approached the bar, Sophie gasped, not trusting her eyes. Wound around Buster's neck and shoulders was a huge snake, its large head resting against Buster's cheek. Several women were taking selfies standing next to Buster, who didn't seem to mind, a shouted beer being the price for the unique photo opportunity.

'Jack! What a pleasant surprise,' said Buster as Jack walked up to him and extended his hand. 'I heard you were in town.'

'It's been a while. Let me introduce you to Sophie. She would love to meet Olive.'

'Ah. The conductor lady. Rusty told me about her. Pleased to meet you, Sophie,' said Buster. 'Would you like to hold her? She's very friendly. Loves people.'

Looking alarmed, Sophie took a step back.

'Come on,' said Jack. 'She's harmless. I'll take a photo for the family album. Something to talk about when you get back to Vienna.'

'If you say so,' said Sophie, rising to the challenge as Buster began to unwind the huge python, and then placed it carefully around her shoulders, much to the delight of the excited crowd, who began to clap.

'You wanted adventure,' teased Jack, taking photos with his iPhone.

'Yes, but—'

'Hold still. That's a good one! The conductor and the snake. That should impress any orchestra. You'll be viewed with new respect.'

'I don't believe I'm doing this,' mumbled Sophie. To her surprise, she was enjoying herself; the warm, not unpleasant sensation of the snake resting against her neck was not what she had expected. After that, Olive returned to the bar and wound herself around one of the posts to give Buster a chance to enjoy his well-earned beers. This was a well-known pub ritual that was repeated almost every night.

'Any more surprises?' asked Sophie, laughing, as she followed Jack back to their table.

'You should have a dance with some of the blokes. They're dying to have a go, but are too shy to ask. You're quite a celebrity now, snake lady. Especially after Olive ...'

'I thought I'd find you here,' said Simpson, sitting down next to Jack.

'Andrew! Great to see you. Can I get you a beer?'

'A little later.' Simpson pointed to Sophie dancing with a handsome young drover. 'She's certainly having a great time.'

'She is. That's why I brought her here. There's nowhere else quite like this.'

'I have to talk to you.'

'Oh? What about?' said Jack, turning serious as he recognised the concern on Simpson's face.

'A favour.'

'What kind of favour?'

'You're leaving on *The Ghan* tomorrow afternoon, right?'

'Yes, I told you.'

'That means you will be in Coober Pedy the next morning.'

'Correct. Is there a problem?'

'Could be.'

'What about?'

'I'll have that beer now, and I'll tell you.'

Deep in thought, Zac Markovich, the publican, sat on the veranda above the courtyard, and watched the revellers on the dance floor below. Ordinarily, he would enjoy observing the action below his flat because it meant rivers of money were flowing into the cash registers of his pub, but not that evening.

The phone call he had received earlier from one of his men running the Drover's Retreat opal claim in Coober Pedy had made him restless. If what the man had told him could be believed, then an extraordinary opportunity was hurtling towards him that required an urgent decision and, more importantly perhaps, immediate action. And Markovich was certainly no stranger to taking risks and advantage of unexpected opportunities, regardless of which side of the law may be involved.

After the sudden, violent execution by a rival gang of the Wizard – the notorious president of the Sydney-based Wizards of Oz outlaw motorcycle club that had owned the pub a few years earlier – Markovich saw an opportunity: he stepped into the vacuum left by the unexpected demise of the Wizards of Oz, and took over the running of the pub.

The licence and the title were already in his name, albeit on trust for the motorcycle club. It was therefore only a small, logical step, to assume full ownership, which is exactly what Markovich had done. But it hadn't stopped there. Markovich set up the Desert Raiders, a new outlaw motorcycle club operating out of Alice. This was a shrewd move with huge, far-reaching opportunities to enter the drug business – big time.

Over the years, Markovich, a born leader with extensive military experience from the Kosovo war, had managed to establish a lucrative criminal empire supplying illicit drugs to Outback Australia by using the Desert Raiders as cover, and recruiting long-distance truck drivers as part of the supply chain.

With the huge amounts of money involved, Markovich branched out and used corrupt police officers and young, mainly impressionable Aboriginal ex-convicts in Alice, to expand his business interests, and infiltrate vulnerable communities. This had made him the undisputed drug baron of the Outback and, as the feared leader of the Desert Raiders, he could call upon anyone in the network to do whatever dirty work was needed to keep the wheels of drug supply turning, and silence possible rivals and opponents.

The reason Markovich had become involved in opal mining in Coober Pedy was quite ingenious. He used the mine as a money-laundering machine, where small opal finds were sold to fictitious entities for inflated prices, to complete a complex corporate purchasing path that 'cleaned' dirty money, and returned it to respectable entities based overseas as 'legitimate' profit.

While dealing with small opal finds made the procedure tedious and time consuming, a really big find could change all that and potentially clean millions in one, bold transaction. As Markovich was in desperate need of 'clean' money to keep his operations going, especially as he had recently come to the attention of the tax department, such an opportunity appeared a godsend.

Feeling calmer because he could see a way forward, Markovich called Goran, his chief of security and sergeant-at-arms, and asked him to come to see him urgently. Goran lived in a caravan just out of town and was never far away. Twenty minutes later, Markovich could hear the unmistakable roar of Goran's bike approaching in the street below. Goran parked his huge chopper in front of the entrance, clipped his helmet to the handlebars, and walked into the pub.

Goran's intimidating aura turned heads and instilled fear wherever he went. Almost two metres tall, in his fifties with greying hair pulled back and tied into a long, plaited ponytail that almost reached to his waist, he radiated aggression and power like a cage fighter. His massive, tattooed arms and shoulders had expanded considerably during years of pumping iron in prison. Dressed in faded jeans and a leather vest that barely covered his huge, hairy chest, he looked like a man who could crush a human skull with his bare hands.

As the sergeant-at-arms of the Desert Raiders he was known as 'Moloch', after the mysterious bull-headed biblical idol endowed with super-human strength and agility. Goran's hand-to-hand combat prowess was almost legendary, and commanded unconditional obedience and respect. As far as Markovich was concerned, Goran was the perfect enforcer and right-hand man. The only things that didn't fit were his handsome face and cornflower-blue eyes, which seemed to belong to a much younger, gentler man. Yet there was nothing gentle about Goran, a former rebel fighter from Kosovo.

As soon as Goran entered the pub, surprised patrons moved out of his way as two security guards rushed over to him and spoke to him deferentially. After all, he was their boss.

'Zac wants to see me,' barked Goran and walked to the staircase at the back of the room leading to the first floor. The staircase was barred by a massive iron grate, which one of the security guards unlocked as Goran approached.

Goran could see Markovich sitting on the veranda and walked outside to meet him. 'You wanted to see me?' he said and pulled over a wicker chair. 'What's up?'

Markovich handed Goran a can of beer and watched his friend as he opened the can and drank. He always felt calmer with Goran by his side because he was the only man he could totally rely on and trust with his life.

'I just had a call from our mine in Coober Pedy.'

'What about?'

'Not quite sure yet, but if what I've been told is true, we have a huge opportunity landing at our feet to turn a massive profit. If we play our cards right and act quickly.'

'I'm listening.'

During the next fifteen minutes, Markovich told his friend what that phone call had been all about, and explained why it could make such a huge difference to the fortunes of their drug business.

Goran listened without interrupting and kept playing with the gold earring in his left ear. This was a nervous habit that helped him concentrate.

Markovich sat back in his chair and looked at his friend. 'So, what do you think?'

Goran took his time before replying. 'We should go and have a look. This isn't something we can do from a distance,' he said, 'or rely on others.'

'I agree. I know it's a long way, but definitely worth a go. Let's keep this under wraps for now, and drive to Coober Pedy to investigate this extraordinary situation.'

Nodding, Goran lifted his beer can. 'Let's do that. Cheers!'

Coober Pedy: Yurlunggur Mine

Suspicious by nature, Jimmy had been carefully watching Toby all day. After the ugly confrontation that morning, Jimmy knew he had to be careful and watch his back. How Toby had managed to follow him down into the abandoned mine shaft in the middle of the night and observe his opal find was still a mystery Jimmy was trying to come to terms with.

But of greater concern by far was the confrontation in the morning, and the crazy proposal Toby had put to him. Toby had bragged he knew all about the stunning opal Jimmy had found, and suggested they should abscond with the precious gem and make their way to Adelaide to sell it, split the proceeds and start a new life.

Feeling worried and uneasy, Jimmy had decided to call Simpson for advice, especially as his refusal to participate in the crazy scheme had been met with a violent outburst by Toby and some angry, albeit incoherent threats.

Simpson was sitting on the terrace behind his house enjoying a cup of tea, when another call from Jimmy came in.

'Calm down,' said Simpson, 'and start from the beginning.'

'I already told you that he saw me dig the opal out of the rock face during the night.'

'You did. You also told me about the angry argument you had with him this morning.'

'Yes, but that wasn't all,' said Jimmy, sounding worried.

'What do you mean?'

'Toby spent a lot of time in the mine next door ...'

'The one run by the boys from the Drover's Retreat?' Simpson realised at once this was bad news. Toby had worked for the Desert Raiders in the past; it was that association that had got him into trouble in the first place and sent to prison.

'Yes. As you know, they're a rough lot and often cause trouble.'

'Tell me about it.'

'Toby's been acting strange all day. I think he's up to something, and I think it involves the boys from the Drover's Retreat mine.'

'Could be. Where's the opal now?'

'Hidden safely in the old mine shaft. Only I know where it is. Toby didn't see me hiding it, that's for sure. Otherwise ...'

'Good. For now, act as if nothing has happened, and should the subject come up with some of the others, deny everything about the find. Say that Toby must have been mistaken.'

'Not sure if that will be enough. It's crucial that word about the find doesn't get out, because if it does, you know what would happen.'

'I understand. Pandemonium! Just do this for now and try to keep the lid on it. Help's on its way.'

'What do you mean?'

'A good friend of mine is travelling on *The Ghan* and will arrive in Coober Pedy in the morning. I told him all about the situation. He will come to see you. Discuss everything with him. You can trust him like you trust me.'

Feeling a little better, Jimmy took a deep breath. 'And you think this could help?'

'It could. The man who's coming to see you is one of the smartest and most resourceful chaps I've ever met. He'll come up with something.'

'What's his name?'

'Jack Rogan. He was the man who rescued Anna Popov all those years ago, and played an important part in the downfall of the Wizards of Oz that I told you about.'

'Oh. And he's on *The Ghan* right now?'

'He is.'

'Coincidence?'

'Perhaps it's more than that.'

'What?'

'He's a man of destiny.'

'Really? I'll do what I can. I just hope he won't be too late. Toby's bad news and I'm sure he's up to no good.'

'Stay calm. The train's on its way, and so is Rogan.'

'I'll try.'

Boarding *The Ghan* Wednesday 25 May

After admiring the spectacular desert scenery and black-footed rock wallabies at Simpsons Gap in the stunning West MacDonnell Ranges just outside Alice, it was time to prepare Sophie for her next outback adventure.

'Where to now? Are you going to tell me where we're going, or are you trying to kill me with suspense?' asked Sophie as Jack was putting their luggage into the boot of a taxi. 'May I remind you this is already Wednesday, and I have to be in Adelaide for a concert on Saturday? If I don't show up, I might as well throw away my baton, kiss my career goodbye, and apply for a job in the Drover's Retreat.'

'I'm sure it won't come to that. Patience, please. All will be revealed shortly. You're in for a big surprise,' said Jack, smiling. 'On the other hand, a job in the pub could be interesting. The conductor pulling beers, watched over by a giant snake ...'

'I've already had so many surprises on this trip, I'm not sure I'm quite ready for another one just yet.'

'You will be, trust me. This is a big one. The highlight of your trip. What you're about to experience is unique and rather exciting by world standards. I had to call in many favours to make this possible at such short notice,' said Jack. 'Travellers have to book months in advance ...'

'I see. More mates in the right places, I suspect?'

'Something like that. Ah, here we are already.'

Sophie looked out of the window. 'A *railway station*?' she said. 'Out here?'

'Aha.'

'We are catching a train? Are you serious?'

'We are. Not just any train, but the legendary *Ghan*.' Jack pointed ahead. 'There it is, waiting for us,' he said and pointed to a string of shiny, stainless-steel railway carriages stretching into the distance.

Powered by two gigantic four-thousand-four-hundred horsepower diesel electric locomotives, this mighty train was almost a kilometre long, with three hundred lucky passengers on board, and fifty staff to look after them. With several restaurants and bars, and luxury cabins for privacy and relaxation.

'One of the great railway journeys of the world ...'

'Good heavens!' said Sophie as Jack explained. 'All this in the middle of a desert?'

'That's what's so remarkable about it. The scenery is stunning, as you will see, especially the colours. More shades of red and gold than you can imagine, particularly at sunset. This train left Darwin, about one thousand five hundred kilometres to the north, yesterday, and will take us all the way to Adelaide, fifteen hundred kilometres to the south.'

'Incredible! Just when I thought things couldn't get any more exciting, especially after Uluru, the helicopter flight over Kata Tjuta, and those cute rock wallabies at Simpsons Gap, you surprise me again!'

'I promised you adventure, and this train is all about adventure, believe me. Come, let's settle into our compartment, and then have a drink at the bar. The train leaves in an hour.'

'You're on!' said Sophie, snuggling up to Jack sitting next to her as the taxi approached the drop-off area.

'Better than conducting an orchestra?'

'Close.'

On the platform, a perky young woman wearing smart khaki shorts and matching shirt – her broadbrimmed Akubra hat a nice Aussie outback touch – welcomed Jack and Sophie and showed them to their Platinum Service compartment.

'Look at that!' said Sophie and pointed to the ice bucket and bottle of champagne on the small table by the window. 'This is some train.'

'Sure is,' said the young woman, smiling. 'Your restaurant and bar are in the next carriage. 'The bar is open now, and dinner will be served at seven pm. While you're having dinner, we'll prepare your bed. The seats over there fold down and turn into a double bed; very comfy. Your private bathroom is just through there. Any questions?'

'No, thank you,' said Jack and reached for the bottle of champagne. 'I've been on this train before. I know the drill.'

'In that case, I'll leave you to it. I'm your personal attendant. My name's Sally. Call on me any time. All part of the Platinum Service. I'm never far away,' said the young woman and left the compartment.

Sophie sat down by the window, picked up *The Ghan* brochure on the table in front of her, and began to read while Jack opened the champagne.

'*Named after the nineteenth-century Afghan camel drivers who helped explore the hostile interior of the continent, construction on a railway line from Adelaide heading north into the desert to Alice Springs began in 1878 ...*' Sophie read aloud.

'Work on the line here in Alice began in 1923, but it took until 1929 to complete the last leg from Adelaide,' Jack continued, who knew it off by heart. 'Until then, passengers had to travel by camel to reach Alice from the end of the line. At that time, steam trains were used, which made the journey even more difficult because of a lack of water and mechanical problems due to distance, not to mention the extreme heat, which made the tracks buckle. A little different from what we are doing right now, don't you think?' said Jack, letting the champagne cork pop.

'Agatha Christie would have loved it,' said Sophie.

'Sure. A little different from the comforts of the *Orient Express*, but just as exciting. Full of romance, rustic charm and adventure, and – who knows? – perhaps even danger. In many ways, perhaps even more so,' said Jack.

He filled up two glasses and handed one to Sophie. 'Here's to one of the great train journeys on the planet. People come from all over the world to experience this. Wait until the train pulls out of Alice and we enter the desert, which begins just out of town. The scenery is simply stunning, especially at sunset. Cheers!'

Sophie took a sip, put down her glass and turned to Jack sitting next to her. 'You sure know how to spoil a girl,' she said. 'This trip is like a dream. One of the most exciting things I've ever done. Thanks, Jack.'

'You are most welcome.' Jack held up his glass. 'In many ways, the best is yet to come.'

'Promise?'

'Absolutely. Cheers!'

Dinner on *The Ghan*

After watching the desert colours of red, golden-brown and mauve fade into a brilliant sunset, illuminating the ancient, weathered hills in the distance like a stage, Jack and Sophie left the bar and took their seats at a table for two by the window, set discreetly apart from the other diners in the exclusive restaurant car.

'How good is this?' said Sophie, studying the menu. 'And they manage to cook all this right here on the train?'

'They do.'

'And you say there are three hundred passengers on board?'

'Yes, about that. There are several dining cars and several kitchens. That's why the train is almost a kilometre long.'

'Amazing.'

'But not everyone is dining in the Platinum Club.'

'Ah.'

'The grilled kangaroo steak, or the saltwater barramundi sound nice,' said Jack.

'Not the crocodile?'

'Perhaps a little too exotic. I wouldn't recommend it.'

'You tried it?'

'I have. Not on the train, but in camps in the remote Kimberley up north. Cooked over open fire in the bush. Amazing what you can eat when you're hungry.'

Sophie shook her head. 'You've certainly been around.'

'I grew up on a cattle station in Queensland, remember? You can take the boy out of the country, but not the country ... You know how it goes.'

'You told me. Must have been tough.'

'It was, and in many ways sad; tragic, in fact. My father died a broken man in a boarding house in Townsville, after losing our farm. One drought too many ... nothing left but the bleaching bones of dead cattle. Stark reminders of shattered dreams and failure. I was in Afghanistan at the time; almost didn't make it to the funeral.'

Sophie nodded. 'Many Aboriginal friends?'

'Yes. Most of the drovers who worked for my father were Aboriginals, but there was one who was my mentor and friend. He died only a few years ago,' said Jack with sadness in his voice. 'We had a special bond. He came to my father's funeral and helped me carry the coffin. He and I were the only ones attending. Sadly, my father died a lonely man, defeated by a harsh life.'

Sophie listened in silence.

Jack sighed and shook his head. 'But enough of that! Let's eat.'

'Good idea. I think I'll have the barramundi,' said Sophie, tactfully changing the subject.

'Good choice.'

Something during the splendid dinner told Jack that the time was right to ask Sophie the one question he had been dying to ask her since their first meeting at the Sydney Opera House. Perhaps it was the sumptuous food and the excellent wine, the intimate lighting and ambience, or the almost surreal feeling of travelling by night through an ancient desert at high speed on a luxury train that prompted him to broach the subject.

Jack reached for Sophie's hand, and for a while just listened to the monotonous, yet strangely reassuring clickety-clack of the steel wheels running along the rails as the carriage kept swaying ever so gently on its axle like a cradle, the sophisticated shock absorbers ensuring not a drop of wine was spilled, even when the train slowed down or went into a turn.

'I've been meaning to ask you this for quite some time now,' began Jack softly, 'but somehow it was never the right moment.'

Sophie looked at Jack, surprised and a little alarmed. 'Oh? But now it is?'

'I think so.'

'Well?'

'What would you say is the most important quality you have that has propelled you to the top of your profession, and allowed you to succeed in such a male-dominated field like conducting?'

Taken a little aback by the unexpected question, Sophie began to smile, and for a while she also listened to the rhythmic clickety-clack of the undercarriage, a sound that allowed her to see things others couldn't: it was the colour blue.

'Too direct?' asked Jack, afraid he had gone too far.

'No. It's just …'

'What?'

'No-one has actually asked me that question. Not in the way you put it.'

'I find that surprising, and I completely understand if you don't wish to answer it.'

'Because it's too personal?'

'Something like that.'

Sophie began to laugh. 'In some ways, you are so refreshingly naïve, Jack. Too *personal*? Really, Jack! I put it down to country-boy shyness. You can't take the country, et cetera, et cetera …'

'You don't mind, then?'

'No, not at all. I'm just a little curious. Why do you want to know?'

'I started out as a young war correspondent in Afghanistan. Many years ago. During that time I saw certain things that made me lose …'

Jack paused, searching for the right words to articulate what he was trying to say.

'*Faith?* In people?'

'Exactly. I was injured in a helicopter crash. Quite badly. There was a lengthy rehabilitation involved. I have a few scars. Would you like to see them?' said Jack, introducing some good-natured humour into the conversation by pointing to his abdomen and chest.

'Not right now. Maybe later,' said Sophie, a sparkle in her eyes.

'I've had a lot of time to think, and I've been searching ever since. Trying to understand—'

'Human nature? Character?'

'Something like that. After I dusted myself off and could walk again, I turned to writing. During my career as a writer that followed, I've met some of the most inspirational, talented and uplifting people, but at the same time, I've crossed swords with some of the lowest, most evil characters you can imagine. Dregs of humanity. I've been trying to understand and reconcile these two opposing sides of the human condition ever since.'

'And an answer to your question could help?'

'I believe it could.'

'All right then, I will answer your question this way: I have a special gift; something rare and unique that has defined not only my life, but also made me who I am. Benjamin has it too and he recognised it in me, nurtured it, and made it blossom.'

'What is it? Tell me.'

'There are two parts to this gift. The first part is absolute, or perfect pitch. Many of the great composers had it: Mozart, Handel, Beethoven, for instance, as did some of the great singers: Maria Callas, Ella Fitzgerald, Bing Crosby.'

'What exactly is absolute pitch?'

'It's the ability to identify any musical note by name simply by hearing it, and without reference to any other notes.'

'And the second part?'

'That's a little more complicated. It's called synaesthesia. Simply put, synaesthesia is a unique blending of the senses when you experience one of your senses through another, like tasting shapes, or feeling sounds, or hearing colours. In my case, when I hear music or certain sounds, I see colours. When Benjamin hears music, he sees shapes. Does this make sense?'

'Not really.'

'It's difficult to explain this to someone who has never experienced it, but there are many examples in art, especially music – even in literature. It's often closely linked to creativity, which allows us to see the world differently.'

'And this is helpful in being a conductor?'

'Yes, hugely. It allows me to experience and interpret music in unique ways, which I then process and translate, convey to individual musicians, and ultimately to the orchestra as a whole. It's a complex process that influences and shapes the entire performance.'

Sophie paused, collecting her thoughts.

'The performance itself is only the tip of a musical iceberg,' she continued. 'Everything I've mentioned so far is the large bit below the surface you can't see, but makes it all float.'

Sophie smiled when she saw the bewildered expression on Jack's face. 'You did ask.'

'I did. Wow! I think I need a musical life vest to keep my spinning head and confused senses above water here, before I see red and drown in a sea of psychedelic notes!'

'A musical life vest?' said Sophie, laughing. 'That's a good one!'

'Seriously, what's it like to be in charge of a symphony orchestra?' asked Jack.

'Intoxicating. A feeling difficult to put into words. It's a position of great power and responsibility. Just consider this: you have the undivided attention of a hundred-or-so talented musicians waiting for your signal, your guidance, which will shape the entire performance. A hundred beating hearts and focused minds, each contributing a vital part to what will, under your direction and vision, come together as one piece of music, with all its subtle nuances and tonal shapes conceived by the composer who created it, but you are at that very moment privileged to perform; to *bring to life*. Does this make sense?'

'Very much so. As you say, it must be an extraordinary feeling. I cannot think of another example of something similar. Something that can bring to life ideas and emotions put down on paper centuries ago, through the participation of living and breathing human beings acting in unison to recreate those very ideas and emotions in real time, and communicate all this to others through music. This is a unique experience of great beauty. Perhaps as close as one can get to immortality.'

Sophie looked at Jack, surprised. 'You put this beautifully, you know. I don't think I've ever heard it expressed so well. You're very perceptive, and a gifted wordsmith.'

'Coming from you, thist is quite a compliment.'

'It's meant to be, but please remember, the conductor is only an interpreter of someone else's genius. The conductor is not the

41

composer, the *creator* of the music. That's why someone like Benjamin is the real genius here. He's the complete package: composer, virtuoso, musician and conductor. All in one. I'm in awe of him.'

'And he of you,' said Jack. He sat back and looked pensively at Sophie. 'I have one more question.'

'Go ahead. I have already bared my soul. There can't be much left.'

'When and how did Benjamin discover you?'

'Ah. That's quite a story.'

'Do you mind?'

'No. In light of what we've just discussed, you should know. You'll see why in a moment.'

'I'm intrigued.'

'In a way, I owe it all to my brother, Wolfgang. My twin brother—'

'You have a *twin*?' interjected Jack, surprised.

'I do. And he's the reason I met Benjamin in the first place.'

'How come?'

'Ah. Wolfgang has the same gifts.'

'Perfect pitch and – what did you call it?'

'Synaesthesia. And a lot more. He has another gift.'

'What kind of gift?'

'A heavenly voice. He was a boy soprano until his voice broke. His first performance of note was at the tender age of nine. He sang "Silent Night" on Christmas Eve in front of the Silent Night Chapel in Oberndorf.'

'Isn't that the village where Gruber and Mohr composed that wonderful Christmas carol?'

'Very good. It is. Our family farm is just outside Oberndorf, near Salzburg. Fourth-generation Alpine dairy farmers. That's where I grew up. The village priest played the guitar that night. I remember it was very cold and snowing outside. My brother's voice was truly outstanding; angelic, people used to say. It moved them to tears – still does. To cut a long story short, the priest took Wolfgang to Salzburg and introduced him to the archbishop. When the archbishop heard Wolfgang sing "Lascia ch'io pianga" from Handel's opera *Rinaldo* –

quite a feat for a nine-year-old – he was blown away. He said when he heard Wolfgang sing, the clouds of earthly existence parted and he could glimpse heaven. A scholarship was arranged, and young Wolfgang went to study music at the Mozarteum University in Salzburg. As a *nine-year-old*; imagine! His career took off almost immediately and he gave recitals first in Salzburg, and then Vienna, virtually straight away. He specialised in baroque arias.'

'So much for Wolfgang, a child prodigy. But what about you?' said Jack.

'My brother and I had a special bond, as twins often do. We were very close; still are. He's now a countertenor, but he performs entirely in the falsetto register, which is quite rare. He has an outstanding repertoire and travels the world.'

Sophie paused, lost in thought as she stared out of the window and watched the darkness gliding past.

'I too had a good voice and we often performed together,' she continued. 'Like Wolfgang, I also began to study music at the Mozarteum at an early age. Looking back, I'm sure I only got a place at the prestigious university because of Wolfgang. I learned to play the piano, but Wolfgang was the star, no doubt about it. I was merely the supporting act. The other twin.'

'I see. So, what happened?'

'One day, several years later, Wolfgang and I performed Pergolesi's "Stabat Mater" at the Salzburg Festival. A very moving piece that showed off Wolfgang's voice to perfection. "Stabat Mater" is all about Mary and her suffering during the crucifixion of her son, Jesus Christ. It's based on a thirteenth-century hymn attributed to Jacopone da Todi, or Pope Innocent III. It was also one of the archbishop's favourite pieces of music. No doubt that was the reason it was included in the program in the first place. A fortuitous choice, as it turned out. Especially for me.'

'How come?'

'Wolfgang and I were known as the Ritter Twins and we often performed together. Our voices had a unique quality, you see. A perfect blend rarely seen. As it turned out, Pergolesi's "Stabat Mater" was also one of Benjamin's favourites. That, and Wolfgang's heavenly, and by then quite famous, voice, were the reasons he attended the concert. He told me so years later. After the performance, Benjamin came backstage and talked to us. Needless to say, we were very impressed. Here was this famous man – one of the main attractions of the festival – who wanted to meet us. We got talking, and it all went from there.'

Sophie smiled as she remembered the meeting.

'I told him that I wanted to become a conductor. Herbert von Karajan, the legendary conductor, who had also studied at the Mozarteum, was my idol, you see. This seemed to impress Benjamin. For a young woman to have aspirations to become a conductor was almost unheard of at the time, especially in conservative Salzburg. I can still remember exactly what he said to me.'

'Oh? What did he say?'

'Moments of genius come uninvited.'

'That's some statement.'

'It sure is. I didn't quite understand what he was telling me at the time, but it became clear later.'

'He told you to trust your instincts and follow your star?'

'Yes, that's exactly what he was telling me. Benjamin stayed in touch and became my mentor. And the rest, as they say, is history. So, here we are.'

'I'm sure there's a lot more to this story you're not telling me. Benjamin must have recognised something special in you, something extraordinary?'

Sophie shrugged coquettishly. 'Perhaps ...'

Before Jack could ask his next question, the host in charge of the dining car invited the guests to return to the bar in the Outback Explorer's Lounge for a surprise.

Storytelling on *The Ghan*

'Ladies and gentlemen, as we are travelling through this ancient land, one of the oldest cultures on the planet has called home for millennia,' began the host after the guests had settled comfortably into their leather seats, 'it is my privilege and pleasure to introduce to you a remarkable man.'

The host paused for effect, to let the anticipation grow.

'He's an Aboriginal elder, a storyteller, who will now entertain you with Dreamtime legends that are part of his cultural heritage, and explain the complex connection between his people and the land, Indigenous values, and spiritual beliefs reaching back thousands of years. Please welcome Ulungura, an elder of the Arrernte people.'

Subdued applause rippled through the carriage as a handsome man with curly white hair and a white beard that accentuated his dark skin, entered the carriage and made a bow before sitting down in a chair at the bar. Looking a little out of place in the elegant surroundings – his striking, furrowed face like a map of a difficult life – he surveyed his audience with eyes that radiated intelligence and curiosity.

'Ulungura is quite a mouthful. Friends call me Uncle Josh,' said the man, his voice surprisingly strong, his manner confident. 'I would like to begin with something many of you would have heard of: the *Rainbow Serpent*. It's a creation story that can be found among most of the hundreds of Indigenous tribes that have traversed this ancient land for thousands of years.'

He has a face that could hold three days' rain, just like Gurrul, thought Jack, smiling, as he listened to the fascinating man take his captivated listeners back into Aboriginal Dreamtime.

'In essence, Indigenous history is oral history handed down from generation to generation. What few people know is that certain volcanic eruptions that occurred in Central Australia thirty-seven thousand years ago, have been incorporated into local Aboriginal creation stories, or Dreamtime stories as they are called, making them the oldest surviving oral history on the planet, still being passed down today. One of those creation stories is the story of Wiradjuri, the Rainbow Serpent.'

Uncle Josh paused and looked calmly through a carriage window to the darkness outside, as something only he could see emerged from the distant past.

'Long before time began and the earth had no features, Wiradjuri, the Rainbow Serpent, who lived underground, began to stir. Wiradjuri was one of the powerful Dreamtime creatures who shaped the earth with the movement of its mighty body, and created hills, gorges and caves, and especially precious, life-giving waterholes, rivers and creeks. Even today, Aboriginal children in the Outback are told stories about the Rainbow Serpent and the importance of how and where to find water, which is so critical for survival in a desert environment.'

An experienced storyteller, Uncle Josh knew how to blend history, facts and traditions with adventure, passion and excitement. He did that by carefully choosing stories he knew his audience would find interesting and entertaining.

After the creation story of the Rainbow Serpent, he changed direction and told the epic Dreamtime story of the Seven Sisters, a very different tale of love, betrayal, lust, passion, death and danger. All lessons of a different kind, handed down through the ages.

After the applause at the end of his storytelling had died down, Uncle Josh asked if there were any questions. One of the guests asked a question about opals. As they were about to visit Cooper Pedy, the opal capital of the world, the next day, he wanted to know if there were any Aboriginal stories about opals and why wearing, or owning one, was supposed to bring bad luck.

Uncle Josh shook his head and replied that he wasn't aware of any Aboriginal bad-luck opal stories.

That's when the storyteller in Jack couldn't help himself. He stood up and turned to face Uncle Josh sitting at the bar. 'If Uncle Josh doesn't mind, I believe I can throw some light on this question.'

'By all means, please go ahead,' said Uncle Josh, obviously pleased to see lively interaction among his audience.

'I have recently come across some fascinating information about this very subject while doing some research for one of my books,' said Jack. 'I'm a writer, by the way.'

Enjoying the attention, Jack paused and looked around the carriage. 'The gentleman is right. There is a certain amount of superstition surrounding opals, and this superstition has its origin in literature. A bestselling novel by Sir Walter Scott published in 1829, to be precise.'

'*Anne of Geierstein*,' a lady sitting in the front called out.

'Correct,' said Jack and pointed to the lady. 'You are absolutely right. *Anne of Geierstein*, or *The Maiden of the Mist*, is indeed responsible for the superstition surrounding opals. Do you know what happened in the novel to give opals such a bad name?'

'Yes. As I recall it,' said the lady, 'it's all about Lady Hermione, an enchanted princess who always wore a beautiful opal in her hair, and was falsely accused of being a demon. When a few drops of holy water were accidentally sprinkled over the dazzling stone, it lost its lustre and Hermione fainted suddenly. She was carried to her chamber and put to bed to rest. However, the next morning it was discovered Hermione had disappeared, and the only evidence left behind was a small pile of ashes on top of the bed where she had been sleeping.'

'Well put, madam. That's some story, don't you think?' said Jack. 'And it had quite an impact at the time. Opal values plummeted and superstition cast a shadow over opals, which, in some way, has lingered to this very day.'

'There's a cursed opal necklace in one of the *Harry Potter* stories,' interjected a man at the back.

'*Harry Potter and the Half-Blood Prince*,' said another.

'Correct,' said a lady, obviously a Harry Potter fan, sitting next to him. 'The evil Draco Malfoy bought it at Borgin & Burkes with the intention of killing Albus Dumbledore, but it ended up with Katie Bell by mistake, who was put under the Imperius Curse by Madame Rosmerta, the innkeeper at the Three Broomsticks.'

'Well, there you have it, ladies and gentlemen, I suppose we'll find out tomorrow if there is indeed some substance to all this when we arrive at Coober Pedy, the opal capital of the world. *You have been warned!*

More subdued applause as Jack turned to Uncle Josh sitting behind him. 'Not as culturally fascinating as the Dreamtime stories, but entertaining nevertheless,' he said.

'Absolutely! Thanks for stepping in. I've certainly learned something new about opals. You're Jack Rogan, aren't you?' said Uncle Josh, lowering his voice. 'The penny dropped as soon as you mentioned you're a writer. I remember seeing you on TV.'

'That's me,' said Jack, smiling. 'There's nowhere to hide these days. Not even out here.'

'The price of fame,' teased Sophie, poking Jack in the ribs with her elbow.

'I knew Gurrul,' said Uncle Josh, turning serious. 'He used to talk about you often.'

Jack looked surprised. 'You knew Gurrul?'

'I did. Very well, in fact. We used to spend time together in the Kimberley, restoring ancient rock paintings, as tradition demanded.'

'Ah. Gurrul loved doing that. He used to spend months visiting sacred sites in the Outback—'

'And telling Dreamtime stories about the paintings to the youngsters sitting around the campfires. He said this connected him to his ancestors.'

'I heard about that. He was a wonderful storyteller. He died quite suddenly a few years ago,' said Jack.

'Yes, in Wyndham. I was there when he died.'

'*You were?*'

'Yes. We had just returned from one of our trips.'

'Well, what a coincidence,' said Jack. 'I scattered his ashes at the Coberg Mission in Queensland, where he wanted to be laid to rest.'

'It was his last wish,' said Uncle Josh.

'This is truly amazing. It looks to me that our paths were meant to cross,' said Jack, a strong believer in destiny. 'Right here, tonight. Can I buy you a drink?'

'Sure. A whisky would be nice.'

'Coming up.'

After spending an hour or so talking with Uncle Josh at the bar, Jack turned to Sophie, who had been following the lively conversation with interest. 'I think we should turn in,' he said. 'It's getting late. We'll have a big day tomorrow. Coober Pedy ...'

'You're right,' she said and stood up. 'We should call it a day. I suppose we'll have a chance to have another chat tomorrow?' she said to Uncle Josh.

Uncle Josh held up his glass. 'You bet,' he said. 'It's been a pleasure meeting you. Sweet dreams!'

'Do you think our attendant has made up our bed?' said Sophie, linking arms with Jack on their way back to their carriage.

'I'm sure she has. It's quite late.'

'In that case, you can show me those scars you told me about earlier ...'

'All right, but I have to warn you, some of them are in rather delicate places.'

'I see. I'm game if you are.' Sophie stopped in front of their cabin door and put her arms around Jack's neck. 'Thanks for a wonderful evening,' she said and kissed Jack passionately.

'As I keep telling you, the best is yet to come,' mumbled Jack.

'In that case, let's go inside and find out if that is so, shall we?' said Sophie and opened the cabin door.

Coober Pedy: Thursday 26 May 6:00 am

Driving through the night and taking turns at the wheel, Markovich and Goran covered the seven hundred kilometres in just under eight hours – record time. They arrived in Coober Pedy just after sunrise and went straight to the Drover's Retreat mine.

The unannounced arrival of Markovich, and especially Goran, made everyone at the mine uneasy and apprehensive. To have the president of the notorious Desert Raiders and his sergeant-at-arms appear just like that, definitely meant something important was afoot. Most likely trouble!

After questioning the man who had called Markovich with the news about the opal find in the mine next door, Markovich took Goran aside.

'It's not much, is it? But where there's smoke there's fire.'

'I agree. And the best way to investigate a fire is at its source.'

'Exactly. So, let's drop in next door and have a chat to Toby and, more importantly, Jimmy, and see what all this means.'

'My thoughts exactly,' said Goran. 'You do know that both Toby and Jimmy used to work for us?'

'I know about Toby, but I had no idea about Jimmy.'

'It was only for a short time; drug deliveries to Darwin. He was just a teenager at the time. He got caught and sent to jail. But I hear he's been a model prisoner and is now out on parole under Simpson's supervision. Simpson and his cronies are involved.'

'Ah, the Aboriginal busybody with the rehabilitation mine ...'

'Quite so. We should tread carefully. Simpson's a resourceful fella. Former cop,' said Goran. 'Friends in high places.'

'True, but he's in Alice and we are right here.'

'Also true. Let's go and have a look, shall we?'

Jimmy and his fellow miners were having breakfast in one of the chambers hewn out of virgin rock at the entry to the main mine shaft at the Yurlunggur mine. Chambers like that, which often served as living quarters for the miners, were the hallmark of Coober Pedy, and one of the main tourist attractions. There was even tourist accommodation available underground in disused mine shafts, which was very popular as it provided a unique, characterful Australian outback experience found nowhere else.

The four young men sitting at a long wooden trestle table froze as Goran entered, filling the chamber with his threatening presence. He had to bend down to avoid hitting his head against the low rock ceiling, making him appear even taller. Markovich, who was just behind him, had to do the same.

'What's for breakfast, boys?' said Goran cheerfully and sat down next to Jimmy on the wooden bench. 'Cornflakes and tea? No cooked breakfast? How about a cuppa? It's been a long drive from Alice.'

'Sure,' said Toby, recovering quickly, and reached for the teapot.

'News travels fast,' said Markovich, 'isn't that right, Goran?'

'Sure does.' Goran turned to face Jimmy sitting next to him. 'Remember me? I gave you your first job not that long ago.'

'I do, and I've regretted it ever since.'

'Did you hear that, Zac? We gave this kid a job and that's what we get in return. What about you, Toby? I gave you a job as well ...'

'You did. I appreciated that. Unfortunately, it didn't quite work out.'

'No, it didn't, but here we are.'

'Why exactly are you here?' asked Jimmy, his mouth dry and his heart beating like a drum.

'We heard rumours ...'

'What kind of rumours?'

'That a large opal was found here the other day.'

'As you said, rumours. Such rumours circulate here all the time. Mines are full of gossip. People live in hope. That's what keeps them going. There was no such find!' said Jimmy.

'Not what we heard.'

'Even if it was true, this mine has nothing to do with you!'

'Oh, but it does. That's where you're wrong, matey.'

'How come?'

'That old, disused mine shaft where you found that large opal the other day, is in fact part of our claim next door.'

Markovich paused to let this bombshell find its mark. It clearly showed just how well informed he was.

'That's *bullshit!*' said Jimmy, digging deep to find the courage to stand up to the unwelcome intruders.

'You think so?' said Markovich. 'Show him, Goran.'

Goran reached into his pocket, pulled out a piece of paper and put it on the table in front of him. 'This is part of a registered claim plan, which shows your mine ... and ours,' he said and pointed to the demarcation line between the two claims. 'This is the disused mine shaft we are talking about, right here.'

Jimmy leaned forward and had a close look at the plan. 'That's part of our mine,' he said, shaking his head. 'The fact that the entry is clearly on our side supports this.'

'That's not the way we see it,' said Markovich, 'is it, Goran?'

'Definitely not. The bottom section where you found the opal is part of our mine. We are claiming the opal find.'

'That's ridiculous!' said Jimmy. 'There is no find!'

Goran reached across the table and put a huge, tattooed hand with a large silver skull-and-crossbones ring on the middle finger, on Jimmy's arm.

'If I were you, I would choose my words more carefully,' said Goran, his tone threatening. He paused and looked around the table. 'I'll tell you what will happen now, lads. Very soon, this place will be full of tourists. *The Ghan* has just arrived. You have until noon – when the tourists leave – to hand over the opal. Is that clear?'

'That's not going to happen!' said Jimmy, looking for support from the others sitting around the table. 'There's no opal, only rumours!'

He realised, of course, that Toby was the traitor in their midst; he was the reason the dreaded Moloch was sitting at their breakfast table, making threats.

'Think it over carefully, Jimmy boy, and discuss it with your friends here, because all of you are in this together.'

Goran stood up and patted Jimmy on the shoulder. 'We'll be back at noon, matey, and please remember, mines are dangerous places. Accidents happen ...'

As Goran walked past Toby he stopped. 'You can have your old job back if you like when all this is over.' Then, lowering his voice, he bent down and whispered *Watch him!* and then walked outside.

'Enjoy your breakfast, boys,' said Markovich as he followed Goran to the exit. 'Better make sure it doesn't turn into your last supper.'

Touring Coober Pedy

The Ghan arrived at Manguri just before sunrise. A railway siding in the middle of the desert without buildings or structures of any kind, Manguri was located some forty kilometres west of Coober Pedy.

'We're here,' said Jack and got out of bed. 'Put on something warm and let's go outside.'

'What are you talking about?' said Sophie, barely awake. 'It's still dark.'

'Not for long. Sunrise in the desert, remember?'

'Oh God. More adventures. I'm not sure I'm up to this.' Sophie pulled the quilt over her head. 'Musicians aren't used to getting up at this hour.'

'Nonsense! You don't want to miss this, trust me. Get dressed and let's go. You've got to see the first rays of the sun rising out of the desert to really appreciate this. And besides, they'll be serving hot bacon-and-egg rolls to keep you warm,' said Jack, lowering his voice, 'at least on the inside. Come.'

'Slave driver,' mumbled Sophie from under the quilt.

'Did you say something?'

'I'm coming.'

'Good. It's just getting light. You're in for a treat.'

Wearing a tracksuit with a blanket wrapped around her shoulders to keep warm, Sophie was watching the sunrise. 'Breathtaking,' she said. 'I've never seen anything quite like it.'

'I told you so,' said Jack, munching happily on his second bacon-and-egg roll as the desert greeted a new day with a display of dazzling colours banishing the darkness. 'The only thing that comes close to this is the Aurora Borealis in Iceland.'

'You've been there?'

'Sure have. A few years ago. Incredible place.'

Sophie shook her head. 'Adventure junkie!'

'Another roll? Here comes a full tray! We have a busy day ahead of us. The buses taking us to Coober Pedy will be here shortly.'

'Oh, why not? If I don't fit into my clothes for the concert, I'll blame you!'

'No problem,' said Jack, handing Sophie another hot bacon-and-egg roll. 'I'm used to living dangerously. Tuck in!'

The short bus ride from Manguri to Coober Pedy took less than an hour. An Aboriginal guide provided an informative commentary and prepared the excited visitors for the attractions to come.

'Those of you who have opted for the walking tour will visit the majestic Breakaways Lookout.' The guide pointed ahead. 'The Breakaways Reserve is just over there. All of this was once an inland sea, and those rugged hills look as if they had broken away from the higher ground. Hence the name: Breakaways.'

'Look at those colours,' said Sophie.

'Stunning, isn't it?' said Jack. 'A kaleidoscope of colours and shapes reminiscent of a lunar landscape.'

'Exactly.'

'As part of your walking tour, you will visit the Umoona Opal Mine and Museum, an underground museum showcasing fossils, an original opal mine, and a home known as the "dugout",' continued the guide.

Jack turned to Sophie sitting next to him. 'A fascinating place, as you will see,' he said. 'We'll also visit an underground Serbian Orthodox church with rock carvings. It's extraordinary! Definitely one of the highlights of the tour.'

'Along the way, we'll drop in at the grassless golf course of Coober Pedy,' said the guide. 'Does anyone know what it is famous for?'

'Yes! Its special relationship with Saint Andrews in Scotland. It's the only golf club in the world with reciprocal playing rights with that iconic club,' said a man at the back, obviously a keen golfer. 'Imagine!'

'Correct. We'll also visit a working mine, the Quest Opal Mine, where an outback lunch will be served. How does all this sound, guys?' asked the guide.

Enthusiastic cheers from the passengers was the response he had been hoping for. Encouraged, the guide continued, 'But that's not all.

After lunch, on the way back to the train, we'll travel alongside the Dingo Fence, or Dog Fence. Has anyone heard of the Dog Fence?'

'It's the longest uninterrupted manmade structure in the world,' said Jack.

'Correct. It's five thousand three hundred kilometres long. It starts in Jimbour on the Darling Downs in Queensland, and goes all the way to the Great Australian Bight in South Australia,' said the guide.

'What's it for?' asked someone at the back of the bus.

'To keep the dingo, a wild dog, out of southern Queensland sheep country. The fence has a long history. It started out as a rabbit-proof fence in 1884 to contain the introduced rabbit population, which had become a terrible scourge. But the dingo, Australia's most cunning predator, turned out to be a far more serious menace to sheep. By 1939, the rabbit-proof fence had been heightened and expanded into a dingo-proof barrier to combat the dingo problem, which was costing the sheep farmers a fortune.'

The guide paused and pointed ahead. 'Well, ladies and gentlemen, here we are,' he said. 'Coober Pedy, the opal capital of the world.'

After spending some time in the museum, which he had visited before, Jack excused himself and told Sophie he had to briefly visit the Yurlunggur mine that Andrew Simpson had been talking about, which was close by. Because he didn't want to alarm her, he only told Sophie that he had to deliver an urgent message from Simpson to the boys working there, and didn't disclose the real reason behind his visit. He told Sophie to stay with the tour and promised he would be back to join her for lunch at the Quest Opal Mine. Before Sophie could question him about this, Jack gave her a peck on the cheek and headed for the exit.

As soon as Jack walked into the Yurlunggur mine, he could sense tension. Two young men were emptying a wheelbarrow full of small rocks, and looked up at him, surprised. One of them was Toby. When Jack introduced himself and asked to speak to Jimmy Bingarra, he was met with suspicion bordering on hostility.

56

'Jimmy isn't here. Why do you want to see him?' asked Toby curtly and walked over to Jack standing at the entrance, his manner not only rude but almost threatening.

'I have a message from Andrew Simpson,' said Jack, trying to appear nonchalant and relaxed.

Toby looked at Jack, alarmed. *Fuck! Must be about the opal*, he thought, biting his lip.

'Jimmy's down in the mine. I'll get him,' said the young man standing next to Toby.

'Thank you,' said Jack, trying to defuse the tension.

'You came on *The Ghan*?' asked Toby, recovering quickly.

'I did.'

'You must be on the tour, then.'

Jack nodded.

'You can give me the message. Jimmy could be a while as he's somewhere deep down—'

'I can wait.'

'Suit yourself,' snapped Toby and turned away.

Moments later, Jimmy walked in, a little out of breath, his hair and face covered in dust. 'Mister Rogan?'

'That's me. Please call me Jack.'

'You wanted to see me?'

'Yes.'

Instead of asking why, Jimmy pulled a handkerchief out of his pocket and began to wipe his face while carefully watching Jack, a worried look on his face.

He's scared, thought Jack, recognising the signs. 'Can we go somewhere quiet?' he asked. 'Outside, perhaps?'

'Sure,' said Jimmy and followed Jack outside. 'Just in the nick of time. Andrew called and told me you were coming. We have a big problem and there isn't much time.'

'What kind of problem?' said Jack.

'We had visitors here this morning. Zac Markovich and Goran, the Moloch, his dreaded enforcer. Do you know who they are?'

'I do. Desert Raiders …'

'And the rest.'

'What did they want?'

'It's all about the opal.'

'It's true, then?'

'Yes. I found a spectacular opal in one of the abandoned mine shafts the other day. Huge. Could be the find of the decade, perhaps the century.'

'How big?'

'Very. Worth a fortune, I'd say. Hundreds of thousands, possibly millions.'

'Wow!'

'Markovich got wind of it and claims the find belongs to him.'

'How come?'

'It's complicated. We have an informant in our midst. Toby. He used to work for Markovich. You've just met him. These men are capable of anything. Trust me, I know. Especially when money's involved. I used to work for them. They gave us an ultimatum.'

'What kind of ultimatum?'

'Hand over the opal, or else ...'

'Or else what?'

Jimmy shrugged.

'Where's the opal now?'

'Hidden, down in one of the mine shafts. I'm the only one who knows where. Markovich will be back later today, expecting an answer.'

'So, what are you going to do?'

'If I don't hand over the opal, I could be dead by tonight. We could all be dead.'

'That serious, you think?'

'With these guys, yes.'

'So, what's the answer?'

'I have to get away from here, quickly! Before it's too late.'

'How?'

'I was hoping you could help me with that. Andrew said you were one of the smartest and most resourceful men he ever met.'

58

'Did he now?' said Jack, smiling.

'Yes.'

'Do you think you could make it to Manguri before the train leaves?' asked Jack.

'I think so.'

'With the opal?'

'Yes.'

'I'll meet you at the train,' said Jack.

'I'll be there.' Jimmy looked like someone who had just been thrown a lifeline moments before drowning in the middle of a storm at sea.

'Make sure you are. The train won't wait for anyone.'

'Understood. I can't tell you how—'

Jack held up his hand. 'You better go back inside and get ready.'

As Jack made his way towards the Quest Opal Mine to meet Sophie, he pulled his phone out of his pocket and called Simpson. What Simpson told him about Uncle Josh, who was obviously a friend, showed Jack the way to get Jimmy on the train.

After the phone call, Jack stopped and surveyed the surreal landscape of Coober Pedy with its subterranean houses, churches and shops, the mounds of discarded rocks and debris the only evidence of the many mines and countless tunnels and shafts carved out of the ancient sandstone by hand, in an everlasting search for riches.

Momentarily overcome by the beauty of the Breakaways shimmering in the midday heat like a mirage, Jack could feel a sense of excitement washing over him. It was a familiar sensation that appeared suddenly and without warning, every time a new adventure came hurtling towards him out of the toolbox of destiny.

Back on *The Ghan*

Jack watched the last of the passengers board the train and turned to Uncle Josh standing next to him. 'He should have been here by now,' he said, sounding concerned.

'Perhaps he couldn't make it,' said Uncle Josh.

'He was desperate.'

'Sometimes being desperate isn't enough.'

As the tourist buses began turning around and leaving, one of them stopped. The back door opened and Jimmy got out, looked anxiously around and walked over to Jack.

'You took your time,' said Jack.

'Markovich and Goran came back early. I had to give them the slip. It wasn't easy,' said Jimmy, his eyes bright with fear.

'Never mind. This is Uncle Josh. You do as he tells you. He'll get you on the train. We'll talk later.'

With that, Jack turned around and walked over to the uniformed attendant waiting at the train with a clipboard in her hand, the loud whistle coming from the engine at the front an unmistakable signal that *The Ghan* was about to leave.

'Come on, son. I got you a job in the kitchen,' said Uncle Josh. 'Do you know anything about cooking?'

'Not much. Only what I learned in the nick.'

'That'll have to do. Let's go.'

Standing behind one of the buses, Toby was watching Jimmy and Uncle Josh get on the train. Cunning and quick-witted, he saw an opportunity to do the same. A van was parked next to one of the carriages, and supplies were being loaded onto the train. Toby hadn't let Jimmy out of his sight all morning and had followed him all the way from the mine to Manguri without being seen. By evading Markovich and Goran, just as Jimmy had done, Toby knew he had burned his bridges and, just like Jimmy, he knew that crossing Markovich and the Desert Raiders had serious consequences.

Toby hurried over to the van. Pretending to be part of the crew, he climbed into the back of the van, picked up a crate of vegetables and carried it over to the train. Because two of the young men doing the same were Aboriginals like himself, he blended in without attracting attention. As the train was about to leave, everything was done in a great hurry. By the time the van was almost empty, one of the young Aboriginals asked Toby to help him carry a crate that was larger and heavier than the others.

'Haven't seen you around before, bro?' said the young man.

'Just started,' replied Toby casually.

'Ah. We're always short-staffed. Kitchen?'

'Yes.'

'All right. This is it. Let's get back on the train and you can help me carry this into cool storage behind the kitchen.'

'No problem, bro,' said Toby, smiling, and helped his new friend lift the heavy crate onto the carriage.

Markovich turned to Goran standing next to him. 'The bastards are on the train, no doubt about it! And you can bet your bottom dollar so is the bloody opal. *Can you believe it?*' he fumed and stormed out of the Yurlunggur mine.

'You mean they've joined forces?'

'Not sure, but both are gone. That I do know!'

After having robustly questioned the two frightened young Aboriginal men waiting for them at the mine about Jimmy and Toby's whereabouts, it had quickly become clear both had absconded. The fact Toby had just disappeared instead of waiting at the mine as arranged made that clear.

Trying to calm himself down, Markovich stopped to consider what to do next. It wasn't often he was outmanoeuvred, but that was exactly what had just happened. And to have been so brazenly defied by two pathetic delinquents in such an important matter was particularly galling.

'These guys didn't come up with this all by themselves, that's for bloody sure,' said Markovich. 'They had help. You heard what the boys just told us. A man called Jack Rogan dropped in and asked to see

Jimmy. He had a message from Simpson. *Bloody Rogan again!* I can't believe it!'

'You've come across him before?' asked Goran.

'I sure have. He and Simpson were involved in my brother Zoran's death at Tunnel Creek.'

'Wasn't that when the Wizard had his accident? The car turned over and he was injured? The Pigeon affair?'

'Yes.'

'But that was years ago. What was Rogan doing here now, do you think?'

'He arrived on *The Ghan* this morning from Alice. I have no doubt this is all about the opal. Must be. This is Simpson's mine, remember? He must be behind it all. Can't you see? It's all connected. And now they're on that bloody train on its way to Adelaide, and we are stuck here like a pair of dumb chooks. Fuck!'

'Calm down, mate,' said Goran. 'Let's think ...'

'You're right. No point in moping. The train would have left by now in any case. Next stop Adelaide, eight hundred kilometres away. There's no way we can make it to Adelaide before it arrives, and meet the bastards—'

Markovich stopped and pulled his phone out of his pocket. 'We can't, but someone else could.'

'What's on your mind?' asked Goran.

'Let me make a couple of calls first, and then I'll tell you.'

'Are you going to tell me what this is all about?' said Sophie as the train was leaving Manguri. 'First, your mysterious disappearance in Coober Pedy, and now this. Who was that Aboriginal boy? What's going on, Jack?'

'Let's go to the bar and have a drink, and I'll tell you.'

Jack ordered two glasses of champagne and sat down at a table by the window. 'Isn't it beautiful?' he said, collecting his thoughts, and for a while just watched the desert landscape glide past as the train accelerated. 'The reason I didn't tell you this earlier is simple enough:

I didn't want to worry you unnecessarily. You know, put a dark cloud into your sunny day.'

'What do you mean?' asked Sophie, frowning.

'There was a problem. Or more precisely, Andrew Simpson had a problem, and I agreed to help. But it's gone away now.'

Jack took a sip of champagne, and then told Sophie the story of the opal find and what had happened in Coober Pedy.

'And that young Aboriginal man I saw you with earlier is the one who found that opal?'

'Yes.'

'And he's on the run because these two thugs you mentioned are after him?'

'That's about it. But thanks to Uncle Josh, he's now safely ensconced on the train, working in the kitchen. Uncle Josh got him a job,' said Jack, grinning. 'Problem solved.'

Sophie shook her head. 'Never a boring moment when you're around, Jack.'

'I'll drink to that; cheers!'

'I think I'll go back to our cabin and have a nap. I'm pooped. And it's all your fault.'

'How come?'

'Need you ask? I've been up since well before dawn, and on the go ever since.'

'But you did see the stunning desert sunrise. And, as I remember it, you did enjoy those delicious bacon-and-egg rolls ...'

Shaking her head, Sophie burst out laughing. 'Now I understand why Benjamin keeps referring to you as that—'

'What?'

'Incorrigible rascal.'

'Not that old chestnut again,' protested Jack, waving dismissively.

'Labels stick because they're accurate.'

'Be that as it may, you did have a good time, admit it!'

'I did, but now I need a little rest so I can keep up with you. With an incorrigible rascal, one never knows what may be lurking around the corner.'

'Is that a complaint?'

'Not at all. Just an observation.'

'That's a relief. After all, you're travelling with an adventure junkie. And may I remind you that you said so yourself.'

Sophie rolled her eyes. 'Tell me about it.'

'I'll stay here for a while,' said Jack.

Sophie stood up, then bent down and kissed Jack on the cheek. 'Thanks for a wonderful day.'

'Glad you enjoyed it, and it's not over yet.'

On her way out, Sophie passed Uncle Josh. 'Do you know where I can find Jack?' he asked.

Sophie smiled. 'Just over there,' she said and pointed to Jack's table. 'I'm sure you'll have a lot to discuss.'

'Drink?' said Jack as Uncle Josh walked over to him.

'Why not? It's been a hectic morning. Full of surprises.'

'Have you seen it?'

'Yes.'

'And?'

'It's truly amazing. I haven't seen anything quite like it. Must be worth a fortune. An opal like this comes along only once or so in a century. No wonder it sent the Desert Raiders into such a spin. I just spoke with Andrew. He has contacts in Adelaide who will look after Jimmy when we arrive.'

'All sorted, then?'

'Looks that way.'

'I spoke to Andrew as well.' Jack handed Uncle Josh a whisky. 'He told me that you're a *kurdaitcha* man,' said Jack, lowering his voice.

'You know what a *kurdaitcha* man is?' said Uncle Josh, surprised. 'Few whitefellas do.'

'Yes. Gurrul told me.'

'Ah. Not many of us left who know all the secret ways.'

'But you do?'

'Yes.'

'Could come in handy from time to time,' said Jack, instantly regretting the somewhat-flippant remark.

'Such knowledge must never be used lightly. The spirit world can be a dangerous place.'

'Of course. Sorry, I didn't mean to—'

'I know you didn't, but now this opal's right here with us on the train, I have to tell you something,' said Uncle Josh, turning serious.

'Oh? What about?'

'Last night.'

'What about last night?'

'Remember when that chap asked if there were any Aboriginal stories about opals, and why owning one was supposed to bring bad luck?'

'Yes. You told him there were no such stories.'

'I did, but that wasn't quite correct.'

'Oh?'

'In fact, opals feature quite prominently in certain Dreamtime stories, but these are sacred spiritual stories only to be retold at particular ceremonies. This is all sacred knowledge, to be shared around the campfires, or communicated through paintings, dances or songs, but only on special occasions.'

'I see. Can you talk about it now?'

'Yes, I believe I can, especially with someone like you, who will understand what I'm about to tell you. I believe this opal has appeared for a reason.'

Jack nodded but didn't reply.

'Opals are part of the *Rainbow Serpent* Dreamtime creation story. Large opals like the one Jimmy found are millions of years old and obviously very rare. They reach back into the mists of time: creation time. They have special powers ...'

'What kind of powers?'

'They can identify and fight evil. Throughout the ages, *kurdaitcha* men have used opals to ward off evil and protect their tribe. In the wrong hands, such an opal can be dangerous. *Very* dangerous.'

'Bring bad luck, perhaps?'

'You could put it that way.'

'You think we may be facing such a situation?'

Uncle Josh nodded, his furrowed face suddenly a map of concern. 'Having just seen the opal, yes, I believe so. It's even shaped like a serpent.'

'That is significant?'

'It is.'

'What do you suggest we do about this?'

'There's nothing we can do, really. The opal has the power here; it will decide. But please keep this to yourself.'

'Of course.' Jack pointed to the empty tumbler in front of Uncle Josh. 'Another one?'

'Why not? Thanks.'

While Jack went to order another drink, the host in charge of the dining car walked up to Uncle Josh, a concerned look on her face. She spoke to him briefly, and then rushed away.

'Well, we didn't have to wait long,' said Uncle Josh as Jack returned with a whisky and a glass of champagne.

'What do you mean?'

'Something's just happened. Something significant that affects us all. The dining car manager just told me.'

'What?'

Uncle Josh leaned forward. 'I'll tell you,' he said, sounding conspiratorial. 'I think the opal has just sent us a signal.'

After hearing the disturbing news, which hit him like a punch in the guts, Jack went straight back to his cabin. He stopped at the door, ran his fingers through his hair, and considered how best to break the worrying news to Sophie.

Sophie was curled up in the seat closest to the window, asleep. She opened her eyes when Jack walked in and sat down next to her.

'Why have we stopped?' she asked, rubbing her eyes. Outside it was getting dark, but it was obvious the train wasn't moving.

'We have a problem,' said Jack softly, coming straight to the point.

'What kind of problem?'

Choosing his words carefully so as not to alarm Sophie too much, Jack relayed what Uncle Josh had just told him.

Sophie sat up, suddenly awake. 'What do you mean ...?'

'We don't know too much at the moment, but I believe an announcement is imminent.'

'Does this mean ...?'

'Unfortunately, yes, it does.'

'Good God! *The concert!* The day after tomorrow!'

'I know.'

'What are we going to do, Jack?' Sophie almost shouted.

'Don't know yet, but I'll come up with something, I promise.'

'This is dreadful. I can already see the headlines ...'

Jack put his arm around Sophie. 'I'm sure it won't come to that.'

'Oh, Jack! After the wonderful time we've had, *this?* How awful!'

'Problems are here to be solved. I'll go and try to find out what I can. You stay here and try to relax.'

No stranger to crises, Sophie recovered quickly. 'You're right,' she said. 'Thanks. I know you'll do your utmost. It's not the end of the world.'

'Certainly not,' said Jack and kissed Sophie tenderly on the forehead. 'I won't be long.'

Stranded on *The Ghan*

Talking animatedly – one hand in the air – Markovich stood in front of the entrance to the Drover's Retreat mine with his satellite phone pressed against his ear. Leaning against the bonnet of his Range Rover, Goran was watching him intently. *At last,* he thought, and lit another cigarette.

For the past two hours, Markovich had attempted in vain to contact one of his drug suppliers in Adelaide, whom he knew well. He was desperately trying to make arrangements for someone reliable he could trust to meet *The Ghan* upon arrival, and track down Jimmy. After a long conversation, Markovich slipped the phone into his pocket and walked slowly over to Goran.

'Any luck?' asked Goran.

'More than you can possibly imagine,' said Markovich, grinning. 'Get the map.'

Goran shrugged and discarded his cigarette. Then he reached through the open car window into the glove box, pulled out a map and handed it to Markovich. 'What's this all about?' he said.

Markovich unfolded the map and put it on the bonnet. 'Come here, I'll show you.'

Markovich traced the railway line from Manguri with his index finger until he found what he was looking for. *'Here!'* he said excitedly. 'You won't believe this!'

'What are you talking about?' asked Goran.

'It's just been on the news.'

'What has?'

'A derailment. Right here, near this bridge. A freight train from Adelaide came off the rails and is blocking the line. Do you realise what this means?'

'*The Ghan* is stuck and can't get through?'

'Exactly! This is a single line all the way to Adelaide. Trains can only pass each other at certain railway sidings like this one here.'

Markovich stabbed his finger at the map. '*The Ghan*'s right here, at this siding near the bridge.'

68

'You're kidding!'

'No. The guy I spoke to just heard it on the news. This is our lucky day, my friend!'

'How far to the bridge?'

'Not far. About two hundred kilometres, I'd say.'

'We could be there in a couple of hours.'

'Exactly. Get in the car!'

Shortly after leaving Manguri, it was quickly getting dark. There was little traffic on the road apart from the massive road trains hauling freight through the Australian Outback during the night, like giant caterpillars crawling through the desert. These huge trucks, with multiple trailers that could be up to fifty metres long and weigh up to one hundred and twenty tonnes each, were often the only way essential supplies could reach remote outback towns. On outback roads, which were often quite narrow and treacherous, meeting such a behemoth could be daunting and dangerous, especially at night, but Goran, who was driving, knew what he was doing and how to pass these monster rigs.

'Over there; *look!*' said Markovich and pointed ahead. '*The Ghan.*'

Lit up like a small town in the distance, *The Ghan* came into view like some surreal apparition melting out of the darkness. Almost a kilometre long, it reminded Markovich of a giant necklace with precious stones sparkling in the night. As they came closer, they could see the twisted outline of the derailed freight train on the other side of a long bridge, with only the huge engine lying on its side lit up at the front.

'That will take ages to move,' said Goran. 'The line will be blocked for days.'

'Perfect, don't you think?' said Markovich. 'A train with everyone trapped inside and nowhere to go.'

'Sure is. How do you want to approach this?'

'Look at all those people! Quite a few cars and trucks have arrived already. Emergency response crew, I'd say. Excellent, we'll blend in.

All we need are those reflective safety vests those blokes are wearing, and bob's your uncle.'

Used to improvising and the unexpected, Markovich could always rely on his military training to show him the way. Goran parked the car some distance from *The Ghan* engines at the front, and they walked the rest of the way. As they walked past a van with its back doors open, obviously a work vehicle, Markovich slipped inside. Moments later, he returned with two safety vests and handed one to Goran. 'Put this on. We've just joined the crew.'

Markovich and Goran followed the lights until they reached the two massive engines at the front of the train. The doors of the first two carriages were open, and workers in overalls were getting on and off the train.

Markovich approached one of the crew working on the undercarriages of the engines. 'What's going on?' he asked.

'We're uncoupling the engines and reversing them. *The Ghan* is going back to Manguri as soon as the line has been cleared.' The worker pointed ahead to the bridge. 'It'll take days to clear up this mess.'

Markovich nodded. 'Makes sense.'

'Lucky about the siding,' said Goran.

'You bet. Without it, turning the engines around wouldn't be possible and the train would be stuck here for days.'

'How long d'you reckon before we can get going?'

'Difficult to say. Couple of hours; could be more. Depends on how quickly they can clear the line back to the Manguri siding. There are a number of freight trains behind *The Ghan*, also stuck. All depends where they are.'

Markovich turned to Goran. 'You heard the man. Let's get on the train and find Jimmy.'

'Needle in a haystack? Look how long this train is. There must be hundreds of people on board.'

'True, but we can narrow down our search,' said Markovich.

'How?'

'Find the honey, and you'll find the bees.'

'What do you mean?'

'I have no doubt it was Rogan who got Jimmy on the train. His idea, for sure. Find Rogan, and we'll find Jimmy.'

'And how are we going to do that?'

'A man like Rogan travels first class. That should narrow it down, don't you think? And besides, I know what he looks like. I've seen his smug celebrity face on TV many times. That too will help, and so will the passenger list. Come on, we'll start here at the front and work our way back. And with all these workers around, we'll blend in perfectly. Watch.'

'No doubt about you,' said Goran, shaking his head and climbing into the carriage closest to the engine. 'Let's go and find the bastard. I only hope he's on the train.'

'We'll know soon enough if he isn't,' said Markovich. 'But I'm prepared to wager ten grand he is. Interested?'

'No way,' said Goran and followed Markovich down the corridor.

While the passengers were eating their dinner in the dining cars, the cabin crew were preparing the guests' beds as usual. Instructions from management in dealing with the disaster had been clear: everything was to appear as normal as possible, to cushion the impact of the crisis and put the passengers at ease. The train's reputation depended on it.

Apart from helping in the kitchen, Jimmy had also been assigned to the cabin crew, which was always short-staffed. All he had to do was help convert the seating arrangements by pulling down the double beds, which were set into the cabin walls. Other crew members then did the rest and made the beds.

As Jimmy was following one of the attendants into a passenger cabin, he caught a glimpse of something that made him pale: a huge man with a grey plaited ponytail reaching down to his waist was coming down the corridor towards him, peering into each cabin.

Jesus! The Moloch! thought Jimmy, a sudden surge of fear making his heart race and head spin, but he had the presence of mind to quickly step into the cabin before Goran came closer and could see him. Jimmy hid behind the door and closed it, but not entirely. Leaving it ajar just a little so he could see into the corridor, Jimmy held his breath as Goran and Markovich walked slowly past, their shoulders almost brushing against the cabin wall.

It's them! he thought, knowing they were looking for him. Jimmy thrust his hand into his trouser pocket, to reassure himself the precious opal was still there. *They're after this.*

Feeling calmer now the imminent danger had passed, Jimmy was frantically trying to work out what to do next. He had to get rid of the stone – now! Hide it, but where? If they found him with it, he was a goner! Then, as often happens in situations of great stress, the agitated mind came up with a solution: *Rogan!* Yes, Rogan was the answer here!

Jimmy knew Jack's cabin number because Uncle Josh had made arrangements to meet there shortly after the train had left Manguri. Fortunately, Jack's cabin was at the front of the train, and Markovich and Goran would have already passed it as they were heading in the opposite direction. Taking a deep breath, Jimmy opened the cabin door, stepped outside and casually joined the passengers coming back from dinner and returning to their cabins.

When Jimmy reached Jack's cabin in the next carriage, he saw that the door was open. The cabin attendant, a young Aboriginal woman he had met earlier, was preparing the bed for the night.

Bugger! Jack's not back yet, thought Jimmy. Returning to the dining car to look for him wasn't an option, because he could run into Markovich and Goran. 'Can I help you, luv?' he said instead and stepped into the cabin.

'Sure, just in time. You can pull down the bed for me,' said the young woman. 'But you have to move the luggage first. Put it into the corner over there.' When Jimmy picked up a duffel bag, he noticed a nametag. The duffel bag belonged to Jack. He put the bag next to a small suitcase in the corner, and then pulled down the bed.

'Thanks; I'll take it from here,' said the young woman.

As Jimmy turned around and began to walk towards the door, he thought he could see Jandamarra hovering above the duffel bag. Mesmerised, he stopped in his tracks and stared at the apparition.

Jandamarra lifted his right hand, pointed to the duffel bag on the floor, and then melted away.

'Something wrong?' asked the young woman.

'No, I'll just move the bag over there, out of the way.'

'Good idea; thanks.'

Jimmy picked up the bag and smiled, because he suddenly realised what Jandamarra had been telling him.

Jack and Sophie had just finished dinner and were having a nightcap.

'Are we really going back to Coober Pedy?' said Sophie.

'You heard the announcement. As soon as they turn the engines around and clear the track, we'll be on our way. In any event, we should be there in the morning, whatever happens. It isn't far.'

'I hope you're right. And then what? I have to be in Adelaide on Saturday.'

'I know. There's a small airport in Coober Pedy. I'll try to get us on a flight to Adelaide. Tight, but it should work.'

'What if it doesn't?' asked Sophie, a worried look on her face.

'One step at a time.'

'You're right. We can't do much more. Certainly not tonight.'

'Another drink?' said Jack and put his serviette back on the table.

'No thanks. I think I'll turn in. It's been quite day.'

'Good idea. Let's go,' said Jack and stood up.

'That's him – over there!' said Markovich as he entered the Platinum Club dining car. He stopped abruptly and turned around to face Goran coming up behind him.

'Rogan?'

'Yes. I'll follow him. You stay here, or better still, go back into the corridor. Stay out of sight and wait for me. Less conspicuous that way.'

'Sure.'

Goran didn't have to wait too long. Markovich returned a few minutes later.

'Cabin 316,' he said. 'Next carriage.'

'What now?'

'Let's step outside to get some fresh air and I'll tell you.'

By the time Markovich and Goran got back on the train, all was quiet. Most of the passengers had returned to their cabins for the night, but the bar was still open and a few guests were enjoying a last drink and chatting to Uncle Josh.

Markovich stopped in front of Jack's cabin and looked around. The corridor was deserted. Satisfied, he looked at Goran standing next to him and nodded. 'Here we go,' he said and knocked on the door. 'Security. Open up, please!'

Jack was lying in bed, reading. Sophie was asleep next to him. Jack got out of bed and answered the door. 'Something wrong?' he said. When he saw Markovich and the towering Goran standing next to him, he immediately sensed danger.

'That depends,' replied Markovich. Before Jack could close the door, Goran stepped quickly forward and roughly pushed Jack back into the cabin. Markovich followed him inside and kicked the door shut behind him.

'Who are you? What do you want?' demanded Jack.

'Nice to meet you at last, Mister Rogan,' said Markovich. 'You were there, at Tunnel Creek, when my brother Zoran died.'

Of course! Markovich the publican and his enforcer, thought Jack, his mind racing. The Desert Raiders that Jimmy had spoken about. *The opal!*

'And so was the Wizard,' said Jack, recovering quickly. 'And we both know what happened to him.'

This guy's good, thought Markovich, appreciating Jack's presence of mind and self-control. 'Let's hope the same doesn't happen to you,' he said.

'What's going on?' asked Sophie, half-asleep. She sat up in bed and stared in surprise at Goran smiling at her.

'We're just having a little chat with your boyfriend,' said Markovich.

'Jack? What's this all about?' said Sophie.

'We'll find out soon enough,' said Jack and turned to Markovich standing next to him. 'What do you want?'

'Straight to the point. I like that. Information. We want information.'

'What kind of information?'

'We know Jimmy Bingarra's on the train. What we don't know is where we can find him. Unfinished business, that's all.'

'I've no idea what you're talking about!' said Jack.

Markovich shook his head. 'This isn't smart, Jack. You want to play games? We can play games; isn't that right, Goran?'

Goran nodded.

Markovich looked at Sophie. 'Goran here is very good at playing games. I will ask again: Where is Jimmy, or more to the point, where's the opal? We know both are on this train.'

Silence.

'Very well. Goran, *playtime!*'

Goran reached into his pocket, pulled out a flick knife, and held it up for all to see. Then he pressed a button on the side of the handle, activating a spring mechanism. A razor-sharp blade inside the handle extended automatically with a click. Slowly, Goran bent down and took hold of a bottom corner of the quilt covering Sophie, and quickly pulled it away. 'Nice nightie,' he said to Sophie, staring at him with eyes wide in disbelief and fear.

Instinctively, Jack took a step towards Goran, but Markovich grabbed him by the arm and held him back. 'Don't pick a fight you can't possibly win,' he said and pulled a gun out of his pocket. 'Just watch.'

Goran kneeled down on the bed next to Sophie, who looked tiny and vulnerable next to the huge man. Then, ever so slowly, he ran the tip of the knife along the inside of Sophie's left leg right up to her thigh, while lifting up the bottom of her silk negligée with his other hand, his touch almost gentle. 'Nice legs too. The rest isn't bad, either, what do you reckon, Zac?'

Stiff with terror, Sophie began to tremble.

'*Stop!*' shouted Jack. '*Enough!* I don't know where Jimmy is, but I know someone who does.'

'Who?' said Markovich.

'Uncle Josh.'

'Is this a joke? Who on earth is Uncle Josh?'

'An Aboriginal elder working here on *The Ghan*. He tells Dreamtime stories to the passengers.'

'White hair and white beard?'

'Yes.'

'We saw him just now in the bar.'

'That's him.'

'And he knows where Jimmy is?'

'He does. He got him on the train and arranged a job for him.'

'Very well. Get dressed, Jack. You and I will go and have a chat with Uncle Josh while Goran stays here with your lovely girlfriend. Understood?'

Jack nodded, well aware that unconditional cooperation was the only way to deal with the situation, for now. He reached for his trousers hanging on a hook behind the bathroom door and quickly got dressed.

By the time Markovich and Jack made it to the bar, Uncle Josh was just leaving and almost bumped into Markovich in the corridor. Mumbling an apology, he looked at Markovich. '*You? Here?*' he said, surprised. 'What are you doing on the train?' Like almost everyone living in Alice Springs, Uncle Josh knew who Markovich was and what he looked like.

'Looking forward to one of your Dreamtime stories,' said Markovich, smiling, his tone sarcastic and threatening. 'Let's go back into the bar and have a chat, shall we?'

Uncle Josh looked pleadingly at Jack. Jack shook his head and pointed with his chin towards the bar.

'I'm just closing,' said the bartender as Jack and Uncle Josh walked in, followed by Markovich.

'No problem. We just want to sit down and have a chat with Uncle Josh,' said Jack breezily.

'Be my guest,' said the bartender and pointed to the empty tables.

'The Dreamtime story I would like to hear more about,' said Markovich, enjoying himself, 'concerns a stunning opal, and a young Aboriginal lad called Jimmy who found it, ran away with it, and ended up on a train. This train. Can you help me with this story?'

'What do you want to know?' said Uncle Josh, well aware of his predicament and the seriousness of the situation. The Desert Raiders, and Markovich in particular, had quite a reputation. And from what Jimmy had told him, Uncle Josh was certain the notorious Moloch wasn't far away either.

'Let's stop beating around the bush,' said Markovich, turning serious. 'No more stories! I know Jimmy's on this train and that he has with him the opal he found recently. The opal belongs to the Drover's Retreat mine, and I want it back. Understood?'

Uncle Josh nodded.

'So, where can I find Jimmy?'

'He should still be in the kitchen, cleaning up. That's his job.'

'Where's the kitchen?'

Uncle Josh pointed to the back of the train. 'Next to the dining car. Just down the corridor.'

'And if he's not there?'

'He would be in my cabin. He's staying with me.'

'Where's your cabin?'

'In the staff accommodation right next to the kitchen.'

'Does this cabin have a number?'

'Yes, 12B.'

Markovich stood up. 'Let's go,' he said and pointed to the exit.

'The kitchen is down the other way,' said Uncle Josh.

'We're not going to the kitchen,' said Markovich. 'We're going back to Mister Rogan's cabin. Now, *move!*'

Inside Jack's cabin it was very crowded, with barely enough standing room for four adults. Sophie was lying in bed with the quilt pulled up to her chin. Goran filled almost half the cabin and Markovich, Jack and Uncle Josh had to squeeze in next to him. Markovich picked up Jack's duffel bag and threw it on the bed to give himself more standing room.

I wonder what he's up to, thought Jack, surveying the almost surreal situation in the crowded cabin. 'What now?' he asked.

Smiling, Markovich opened the bathroom door. 'Step inside, gentlemen, or shall I say, ladies first?' Markovich pointed to Sophie. 'Get out of bed and join them.'

'This is stupid!' said Jack. 'There's barely enough room in there for two.'

'Well, someone will have to sit on the loo, perhaps your girlfriend, and you can stand in the shower, giving Uncle Josh some room at the hand basin.'

'Are you serious?'

'Absolutely. You will stay in there until we find Jimmy.'

After Jack, Sophie and Uncle Josh had squeezed into the tiny bathroom as directed, Markovich closed the door and turned to Goran. 'Block the door with that chair over there,' he said.

Goran did as he was told and wedged the chair against the door handle. 'There's no way they'll get out of there, and there are no windows,' he said.

'Good. Now, let's go and find that bastard!' said Markovich and quickly walked out of the cabin.

Toby hadn't let Jimmy out of his sight after he had accidentally come across him in the kitchen. This happened shortly after Toby had surreptitiously boarded the train in Coober Pedy. Because the kitchen was very crowded and hectic, watching Jimmy from a distance without being seen hadn't been too difficult. However, as the evening progressed and the kitchen staff retired after dinner had been served, and only the clean-up team remained, staying hidden had become more difficult. Months spent in youth detention, and later in prison, had taught Toby to think on his feet and improvise.

To solve the problem, he had come up with an ingenious way to watch Jimmy at work in the kitchen without being seen: by hiding in a small storeroom with the door ajar.

Toby gasped when he saw Markovich and Goran burst into the kitchen and walk up to Jimmy, who was mopping the floor. How on earth did they manage to get on the train? he wondered, disbelief and fear making his head spin.

Apart from two other Aboriginal youths cleaning stoves at the far end of the kitchen, the carriage was deserted. Markovich walked over to them and told them to leave. Because Markovich looked and acted like a man of authority, they left the kitchen without asking any questions and Markovich locked the door behind them.

'Hello, Jimmy. *Surprised?* Bet you are. You should have waited for us at the mine as I asked you to. It would have made things a lot easier, don't you think, Goran?'

'Definitely,' said Goran, coming closer.

Jimmy stood there calmly without saying a word. Because he had seen Markovich and Goran earlier, he wasn't really surprised by the encounter. In fact, he had been expecting it, and was ready.

He doesn't seem to be afraid, Markovich thought, watching Jimmy carefully. How strange.

'Now, Jimmy, you know why we are here. We can do this the easy way, or the hard way; isn't that right, Goran?'

'Absolutely,' said Goran, rubbing his huge knuckles, a clear sign of things to come. A master of violence and intimidation, Goran knew how to create fear, the most reliable tool for getting what he wanted.

'We know you brought the opal with you,' continued Markovich, bluffing, to further intimidate Jimmy. 'All you have to do is hand it over, and all of this goes away; we go away. Simple. So, what will it be?'

'I've already told you, there is no opal, only rumours.'

'Here we go again,' said Markovich, shaking his head. 'This is both boring and stupid, and most important of all, it's wasting our time. I don't like wasting time. I wonder, do you perhaps have the opal on you? Here? Right now?'

'You aren't listening. There is no opal, only rumours.'

'Did you hear that, Goran? Do you believe him?'

'No.'

'*Search him!*' barked Markovich.

Goran stepped forward, yanked the mop out of Jimmy's hand, dropped it on the floor, and then frisked him.

'Nothing here,' he said.

'Pity,' said Markovich. 'Where's the opal, Jimmy?'

Jimmy stood there without moving a muscle and didn't say anything, his body language defiant.

'Have it your way. Goran has wonderful ways to loosen the tongue; isn't that right, Goran?'

'Absolutely,' said Goran, his eyes darting around the kitchen. 'And one of the best is fire.' With that, Goran walked over to the gas stove and lit one of the burners. Then he returned to Jimmy and dragged him roughly by the scruff of his neck across the floor all the way to the stove.

'For the last time, Jimmy, before things get ugly: Where's the opal?'

Jimmy didn't reply, the tension growing by the second.

Kid's got courage, I give him that, thought Markovich and locked eyes with Goran watching him. What if the opal wasn't here at all? Only one way to find out. Markovich nodded. It was the signal to begin.

Mesmerised, Toby watched from the storeroom as Goran grabbed Jimmy's wrist with one hand and put his other hand over Jimmy's mouth to prevent him from crying out. Then, ever so slowly, he brought the palm of Jimmy's hand closer to the burning flame until it was directly above it and just held it there as Jimmy began to convulse violently, the pain almost unbearable. A few seconds later, Goran withdrew Jimmy's blistered hand from the flame and loosened the grip around his mouth. Gasping for air, Jimmy's body went limp and he almost fainted.

'Where's the opal?' repeated Markovich softly. 'Tell me, before it's too late!'

When Jimmy opened his eyes, he thought he could see Jandamarra hovering above the stove, looking at him from above. Slowly, Jandamarra lifted his right hand and put his index finger against his lips.

'*Fuck off!*' croaked Jimmy.

Jesus! thought Toby, holding his breath as Goran pushed Jimmy's hand towards the gas burner for a second time. As excruciating pain once again pierced his brain, Jimmy glimpsed something out of the corner of his eye. A kitchen knife had been left on the stove. Mustering all his remaining strength, he twisted his body towards the stove, reached for the knife with his free hand and grabbed it.

As Goran forced the palm of Jimmy's hand down into the flames, Jimmy thrust the long blade of the knife deep into his tormentor's arm. Goran cried out in pain, let go of Jimmy's hand and looked at the knife stuck in his arm, his face contorted by disbelief and rage. Then he pulled the knife out of his arm, dropped it, and stared at the blood gushing from the deep wound.

When he saw Jimmy looking at him, smiling, Goran lost it. For an instant, he was back in Kosovo fighting the enemy in a forest, violence and death all around him, and only one thought on his mind: survival.

Ignoring the blood and the pain in his arm, Goran put his massive hands around Jimmy's head and twisted it violently to one side, breaking his neck and killing him instantly.

'Nooo, you moron!' shouted Markovich as Jimmy's limp body fell to the floor. 'Can't you see? He was the only one who could tell us where the opal is! But not anymore, it seems,' he added quietly as he looked at Jimmy's body lying motionless on the floor next to the mop, a turned-over bucket and a pool of water. 'All that's left is a problem. A serious one!'

'Sorry. I don't know what came over me,' said Goran, holding his injured arm. Then he walked over to a first aid kit affixed to the wall. While he was attending to his injury, as he had done many times during the Kosovo war, Markovich walked around the kitchen, looking for something. Moments later, he returned with a tarpaulin he had found in the cool room and placed it on the floor next to Jimmy's body.

'How bad is it?' asked Markovich.

'It'll need stitches later, but I've patched it up for now. Bleeding's stopped. I'll be fine.'

'Good. Come over here and help me,' said Markovich.

'Sure ...'

'We can't just leave him here.'

'Of course not. What's on your mind?' said Goran.

'We'll take him outside and bury him. Lucky the train hasn't left yet. Then we go back to the car and drive to Coober Pedy. I'm sure we'll beat the train. Nothing happened here. At least, nothing that can implicate us.'

'Why Coober Pedy?'

'Because of the only lead we've got left.'

'What kind of lead?' said Goran, looking puzzled.

'*Toby*! Who else? As far as we know, he too is on this train, and there can be only one reason for that.'

'The opal.'

'Exactly. And who knows what he's been able to find out. We know Jimmy didn't have it on him. It has to be somewhere on the train, right?'

'Makes sense.'

'And we know Toby's a resourceful lad. With balls!'

'He's that, for sure.'

'As the train is heading back to Coober Pedy, so is Toby, and we'll be waiting for him when he arrives. With a few questions ...'

'I see what you mean. That's brilliant!' said Goran, nodding appreciatively. 'So, this isn't the end of the opal?'

'Not necessarily, but we can't keep looking for it here on the train. Not after what's happened.'

'I suppose not. What about Rogan and his girlfriend locked in the bathroom with Uncle Josh the storyteller?' asked Goran, a sparkle in his eyes.

'They can stay there for now. Someone will free them in the morning and they'll have a lot of explaining to do, but by then we should be in Coober Pedy. Long gone.'

'You're not mad at me?' said Goran, surprised by the calm, rational way Markovich was handling the situation.

'Shit happens. He stabbed you, and you reacted. That's all there is to it.'

'I'm glad you see it that way.'

82

'Now, let's carry him outside and bury him.'

'Right. Let's do that.'

Markovich held up his hand. 'What was that? Did you hear it?'

'What? I didn't hear anything.'

'A whistle. Here it is again! *Shit!* The train is moving!'

'You're right. It is. The burial just went out the window, and we are stuck with a body inside. What are we going to do now?'

'I'll think of something. Let's wrap him in this and put him in the cool room for now until I work out what to do. Quickly! And then we get out of here and lie low! Thank God it's a long train and Coober Pedy isn't far. We should be there by sunrise at the latest.'

Almost paralysed by fear, Toby watched Markovich and Goran come out of the cool room, and then leave the kitchen. After a few minutes, he came out of his hiding place, desperately trying to work out what to do next.

When he walked past the mop and bucket on the kitchen floor, he felt suddenly sick as images of Jimmy's violent murder appeared with alarming clarity. Toby turned away, hoping the feeling would stop, but it didn't. As he began to retch, he rushed to the toilet in the corridor outside and just made it inside before violently vomiting all over the floor.

Return to Coober Pedy: Friday 27 May

Feeling better, Toby washed his face at the basin, and then stepped into the corridor. He realised he had to tell someone what he had just witnessed, but who? Then he remembered Jack.

Simpson sent Rogan, and Rogan's on this train, he thought. Then he remembered something he had overheard earlier: 'What about Rogan and his girlfriend locked in the bathroom?' he'd heard Goran say. What could he have meant by that? Toby asked himself.

Scratching his head, he stopped and listened to the rhythmic clickety-clack of the steel wheels as the train accelerated, the familiar sound jogging his memory as he remembered something else – Markovich's reply: 'They can stay there for now. Someone will free them in the morning.'

As he walked past cabin 316 in the next carriage, Toby stopped. *That's Rogan's cabin!* he thought, as he remembered following Jimmy and an elderly Aboriginal man to meet Jack in his cabin shortly after they had boarded the train. 'Why not? Nothing to lose,' he muttered and knocked on the door.

Jack stood in the shower. 'Did you hear that?' he asked.

'I didn't hear anything,' said Sophie, who was seated on the toilet, still in her nightie and with a towel draped around her shoulders.

'Neither did I,' said Uncle Josh, leaning uncomfortably against the hand basin.

'There it is again; *listen*! Someone's knocking on the cabin door outside. Help!' shouted Jack. 'We're locked in!' He pushed past Uncle Josh and began to hammer his fist against the bathroom door. 'Help!'

In the corridor outside, Toby thought he could hear something. He put his ear against the cabin door, listened, smiled, and then went to fetch the cabin attendant.

'Am I glad to see you!' said Jack when cabin attendant Sally opened the bathroom door, her eyes wide with disbelief and surprise. In this job she had seen many things on *The Ghan*, but certainly nothing quite like this.

'What on earth happened?' she asked as Jack, Uncle Josh and Sophie stepped out of the tiny bathroom.

'It's a long story. Tell you later,' said Jack. Then he saw Toby standing at the door, a worried look on his face, his eyes darting nervously around the cabin.

'He called me,' said Sally and pointed to Toby.

'Seems like everybody's on this train,' said Jack, shaking his head. 'What brings you here, mate?'

'I have to talk to you,' said Toby, fear etched on his young face.

He looks terrified, thought Jack. *I wonder why.* 'Thanks, Sally, we'll take it from here,' Jack said.

'Yes, we'll take it from here,' echoed Uncle Josh, who knew Sally well, to reassure her.

Taken aback, Sally said, 'If you say so. You know where to find me if you need me,' and left the cabin.

'All right, Toby, let's hear it. What do you want to tell me?' asked Jack.

'Something terrible's happened.'

'What?'

Toby took a deep breath and looked at Jack, terror in his eyes. 'The Moloch killed Jimmy,' he whispered after a while, barely able to speak.

After Toby had told them exactly what he had seen in the kitchen earlier, Jack went into the bathroom and got Toby a glass of water. 'Here, calm down,' said Jack and turned to Uncle Josh. 'Do you have security guards on the train?'

'Yes, two. I'll go and get them. You stay here and don't open the door for anyone. Don't forget, Markovich and Goran are somewhere on this train.'

'Understood,' said Jack, opening the cabin door for Uncle Josh and following him outside.

'Let's keep Sophie out of this, if it's somehow possible. She's got to be in Adelaide for a concert on Saturday! Her career and reputation depend on it! And try to keep the bathroom incident quiet if you can. At least for now. *Please?*'

'I'll see what I can do,' said Uncle Josh, nodding his head. 'I know the security guys well.'

'Good. What about Sally?' asked Jack.

'She'll be fine. Leave her to me.'

'Thanks. I can't tell you how much I appreciate this!'

'None of this is your doing, Jack. Wrong place, wrong time, that's all. And then, of course, there's the opal ... the curse,' Uncle Josh added softly, thoughtfully stroking his beard. 'Getting to Adelaide in time won't be easy,' he added. 'There are three hundred frustrated passengers on this train, all trying to work out what to do. It will be bedlam when we get back to Manguri, and there are only a few flights a week with a small local airline out of Coober Pedy.'

'I know,' said Jack. 'I'm working on it. This is quickly turning into the train trip from hell.'

'Better go back inside and lock the door. I'll get the security boys.'

'All right. Thanks, Josh.'

Twenty minutes later, Uncle Josh returned with two sleepy armed guards. It was just after two am.

Jack turned to Sophie sitting on the bed. 'You stay here and don't open the door for anyone; clear?'

Sophie nodded her head. 'You promised adventure; I just didn't realise it would be deadly,' she said sadly.

'Neither did I,' said Jack and gently stroked Sophie's hair. 'I have to go and sort this out. We have to get to the bottom of this and find out what really happened here.'

'Following your breadcrumbs of destiny, as Benjamin used to describe your escapades?'

'Something like that,' said Jack, smiling.

'Please don't forget I have to be in Adelaide on Saturday for the concert,' said Sophie, trying not to sound too anxious.

'Working on it.'

'I knew you would. Be careful, adventure junkie ...'

'Always,' said Jack, pleased to see that Sophie hadn't lost her sense of humour, and followed Toby into the corridor outside.

'It happened right here,' said Toby, pointing to the kitchen floor. He looked confused because the mop had disappeared, the bucket had gone, and there was no spilled water on the floor. 'I don't understand,' he mumbled.

'What don't you understand?' said Jack.

'Everything looks different. There was a mess right here on the floor where it all happened. A mop, a bucket, but it's all gone.'

Jack locked eyes with Uncle Josh and gave him a meaningful look. The two security guards stayed in the background and just listened.

'You say they wrapped Jimmy's body in a tarpaulin and carried it into the cool room over there?' said Jack and pointed to the cool room.

Toby nodded. 'They did.'

'All right. Let's go and have a look, shall we?'

The two security guards followed Jack into the cool room. Uncle Josh walked over to Toby, who was visibly upset. 'We'll stay here, son,' he said and put his arm around Toby to comfort him.

A few minutes later, Jack and the two security guards came out of the cool room, a grave expression on their faces.

Jack shook his head. 'There's nothing in there,' he said.

'There must be!' Toby almost shouted. '*I saw it!*'

'Where exactly were you?' asked one of the guards.

'Over there, hiding in that storeroom.'

The two guards looked at each other. 'You better come with us and we'll write it all down,' said one of the guards and walked over to Toby.

'We'll call the police in Coober Pedy,' said the other guard as he walked past Jack and Uncle Josh. 'And then we'll search the train and try to find those two guys you mentioned. We're not far from Manguri, in any case.'

'What do you make of this?' said Jack, after the guards had left the kitchen with Toby. 'He's either mistaken, making it all up, or someone has been here and covered their tracks.'

'My thoughts exactly,' said Uncle Josh.

'Which one is it, do you think?'

Uncle Josh took his time before replying. 'I think Toby's telling the truth. You saw his reaction, his face ... someone's been here and cleaned up. Don't forget, we are dealing with the Desert Raiders, and we know that Markovich and the Moloch are on the train. That's quite compelling.'

'I agree,' said Jack. 'But what about the body?'

'I know; that's a problem. We'll see. You heard: the guards will start searching the train.'

'That could take forever. This is a huge train! Dozens of carriages, several kitchens, storerooms, luggage compartments. Hundreds of passengers! The body could be anywhere.'

'You saw their body language,' said Uncle Josh. 'I don't think the security boys are taking this seriously, and who can blame them?'

'No concrete evidence, and the only witness is a desperate, young Aboriginal stowaway. A convicted criminal.'

'I know that too. It's a mess, and on top of all that, we'll have to make sure not to alarm the passengers or we'll have panic on our hands, not to mention the sensational publicity. A murder on *The Ghan*? Can you imagine?'

'Yes, headlines around the world, with us right in the middle of it all,' said Jack. 'And newshounds descending on Coober Pedy like vultures for the outback story of the decade. Bedlam!'

'Let's hope it won't come to that,' said Uncle Josh.

'Yes, for Sophie's sake.'

'Let's go back to your cabin and see what happens. We need some time to think.'

'Good idea.'

'We might as well make ourselves comfortable,' said Markovich, stretching out on top of a set of suitcases. Markovich and Goran had broken into one of the luggage storage compartments at the back of the train because it was the safest place in which to hide. 'It's been quite a night.'

'Sure has,' said Goran, playing with his earring. 'I must say, the way you dealt with this was genius.'

'Disposing of the body without a trace?' said Markovich, laughing. 'Yes.'

'Often the simple, most obvious solution is the best.'

'You mean throwing the body off the train and cleaning up the kitchen?' said Goran.

'Precisely. But we did have luck on our side. That always helps. No-one around because it was late, and the kitchen window could be opened. That was key.'

'You're right. Luck favours the bold, as you always keep telling us.'

'It sure does. And should the body be found somewhere out there in the desert, which is by no means certain or even likely, the injuries are totally compatible with a fall off the train – by a stowaway,' Markovich added, raising an eyebrow.

'A broken neck; you're right. So, what's next?'

'Simple really,' said Markovich. 'As soon as the train arrives in Manguri, which won't be long now, we get off. There will be a lot of activity and confusion for sure, with the train coming back and all that. Which means we won't be noticed. I'll ring our mine and one of the boys will come and pick us up.'

'What about Rogan and his friends locked in the bathroom?'

'What about it?' said Markovich, laughing. 'I'm sure they would rather forget all about that, than make a fuss. And besides, We'll be long gone by the time they get out. Game over!'

'You're right. You thought of everything.'

'I hope so.'

'What about the car we left behind at the bridge?'

'We'll send a couple of the boys to go and pick it up. Should take them only a few hours, there and back.'

'And the opal?'

'Ah. Toby, our lead. We'll just wait until he comes to us.'

'What do you mean?'

'We know he's somewhere on this train. Where do you think he'll go once we arrive?'

'Back to Coober Pedy. The Simpson mines.'

'Exactly. He has nowhere else to go. And when he arrives, we'll pay him a visit and find out what he knows. If he knows where the opal is, we'll find it. If not, we'll just drive back to Alice and have a beer in the pub.'

'I'll drink to that,' said Goran, relieved that the problem of Jimmy's unfortunate death seemed to have gone away, thanks to his boss, and he was off the hook.

The abduction

The early morning arrival of *The Ghan* in Manguri was chaotic, with all the passengers desperately wanting to get off the train to somehow continue their journeys. As Markovich had correctly predicted, no-one paid any attention to two men getting into a waiting car and driving off.

'Did you see the cops?' said Goran. 'I wonder what they are after?'

'Who cares?' said Markovich, enjoying himself. It felt good to be a step ahead of the game. 'If it's Jimmy's disappearance that brings them here, good luck! They won't find anything. And besides, these are country cops with little experience in matters like that. Lazy bastards. We've got nothing to worry about, mate.'

'I suppose not. So, what's next?'

'We go back to the mine and wait.'

'For Toby?'

'Exactly.'

What Markovich and Goran didn't see was Toby being taken to one of the waiting police cars for questioning.

The first thing Jack had done upon arriving in Manguri was call Simpson to tell him what had happened during the night.

'What do you think?' Simpson had asked. 'Can Toby be believed?'

'I think so. And so does Uncle Josh.'

'I see. And the police are now involved?'

'They are. The train's being searched as we speak.'

'They won't find anything.'

'What makes you say that?'

'If Markovich and the Moloch are somehow involved, they know how to cover their tracks. And besides, they've got contacts in the police, all the way to the top. We have to be careful.'

'What are you suggesting? We may never find out what really happened?'

'That's a distinct possibility. We are dealing with the Desert Raiders here. They march to a different drum.'

91

'You mean drug money and corruption, not the law?'

'Something like that.'

'Even in a murder case?'

'Yes. These guys are capable of anything.'

'Great! Andrew, I need your help.'

'Go on.'

'Have you got a minute?'

'Sure.'

'I've to somehow get Sophie to Adelaide for tomorrow's concert, but there are no flights; they're all fully booked. And no cars to rent, either. We're stuck here!'

'I see.'

'This is serious. Her career and reputation are on the line.'

'I understand.'

'And this trip was my idea.'

'I can see your dilemma.'

'Can you?'

'Sure.'

'There isn't much time.'

'I can see that too,' said Simpson, smiling on the other end of the line.

'Could you help?'

'I'll see what I can do.'

'Thank you, my friend.'

'For you, Jack, anything.'

Looking bored and smoking a cigarette, Goran stood in front of the Drover's Retreat mine. He had his doubts about Toby coming back to the mine next door, but Markovich seemed certain and was prepared to wait.

As Goran turned around to go back into the mine, he almost collided with two men coming towards him. 'Sorry,' mumbled Goran and stepped aside.

One of the men stopped, looked at Goran – his eyes wide with shock and disbelief – and gasped.

'You all right?' asked Goran.

The man nodded and walked away.

'What was all that about?' asked the other man. 'You look like you've seen a ghost.'

'P-perhaps I have,' stammered the man. He stopped, turned around and watched Goran walk back into the mine. 'Do you know who that was?'

'No; who?'

'Let's go back to our mine and I'll tell you. Call Savo and Dragan.'

'Are you sure, Milan?'

'*Just do it!*' snapped the man. 'I want a meeting, *now!*'

'All right,' said the man, surprised by his friend's outburst. He pulled his phone out of his pocket and made a call.

While there were more than forty nationalities represented in Coober Pedy, Serbs – many of them refugees from Kosovo after the end of the war in 1999 – had formed a tight-knit community, with several mining claims being operated by their compatriots. They had even built a stunning underground Serbian Orthodox church – Saint Elijah the Prophet – carved out of solid rock, which had become one of Coober Pedy's main tourist attractions.

Dragan Mitic, a former police officer and one of the Serbian community leaders, arrived at the mine half an hour later. Savo Ivanovich, his deputy, arrived ten minutes later.

'What's all this about?' asked Dragan. 'You said it was urgent.'

'It is. You won't believe who I just saw,' said Milan, the excitement in his voice obvious.

'Who?' asked Mitic.

'Slobodan Lazarevic.'

Silence.

'The Butcher of Pristina? *You can't be serious!*' said Mitic at last, looking incredulous.

'But I am. I would recognise that monster anywhere. It was him. No doubt about it.'

'What happened?' said Ivanovich.

'He almost bumped into me in front of the Drover's Retreat mine, and then went into the mine.'

'The Desert Raiders' claim,' observed Ivanovich and turned to Milan. 'Describe him to me.'

Step by step, Milan gave a detailed description of the man he had just encountered, including his enormous size and distinctive facial features.

Ivanovich shot Mitic a meaningful look. 'It fits,' he said, nodding. 'I too would recognise that man anywhere. I even questioned him once. He was one of the most wanted war criminals after the end of the war. Then he disappeared ...'

'Where is he now?' said Mitic.

'Inside the Drover's Retreat mine, I suppose,' replied Milan.

'All right. Now listen carefully, guys,' said Mitic. 'This is what we'll do ...'

Jack spent most of the afternoon making phone calls in a futile attempt to secure a flight to Adelaide. He had even spent several hours at the airport, pleading with the staff to let him have at least one seat on one of the few flights to Adelaide. All without success. Uncle Josh, too, had done his best, but to no avail. He had also spent the whole day at the police station with Toby, trying to find out what had happened to Jimmy.

Most of the passengers were stuck on *The Ghan*, waiting for buses to take them either back to Alice, or to Adelaide, but that would take a day or two to arrange because the buses had to travel long distances to reach Manguri.

By the time Jack returned to the train, it was late afternoon. Sophie, who had stayed on the train, was anxiously waiting for him in the bar. As soon as Jack walked in, looking exhausted and uncharacteristically dejected, Sophie knew the answer to the question that had tormented her all day.

Jack let himself fall into a chair next to Sophie. 'I could kill for a cold beer,' he said.

'No luck?'

Jack shook his head.

'No concert, then?' said Sophie, the disappointment and worry in her voice palpable.

'Looks that way, and it's all my fault.'

'Don't be silly. It was an accident that caused all this, that's all.'

'We could have stayed in Sydney and had a good time.'

'You can't reconstruct the past. You of all people know that.'

'Still ...'

'And miss Rosie, and Olive?' said Sophie, a sparkle in her eyes.

'Highlights of the trip?'

'Two of them; there were more. How did you put it: I wouldn't have missed it for—?'

'*Quids.* Yes, great Aussie saying.'

'What's quids, by the way?' asked Sophie.

'*Money.* Aussie slang for Australian pounds.'

'But you have dollars?'

'Not before 1966, we didn't. We had pounds, shillings and pence at that time, until we changed to a decimal currency, the Aussie dollar.'

'Ah. You and your sayings!'

Jack reached for the beer the waiter had put on the table and gulped it down. 'The world always looks better after a cold beer,' he said.

'You sound just like Rusty.'

'A beer heals many wounds in the Outback, inside and out.'

'Is this one of those occasions?'

'Could be, but not all is lost.'

'What do you mean?'

'It's all up to Andrew now. He promised to help, and he's one of the most capable men I've ever met. Anna Popov wouldn't be alive today if it hadn't been for Andrew and his ingenuity.'

'I see. And you think he could help us here?'

'Perhaps.'

'How come?'

'Because of the last thing he said to me this afternoon.'

'Oh? What was that?'

'Hope has wings.'

'Hope has wings? What did he mean by that, do you think?'

'Not sure, but I have an idea because of something similar that happened when we tried to rescue Anna.'

'Are you going to tell me about it?'

'Perhaps later. Andrew said he would call again once he knew more. Let's have something to eat. I'm starving!' said Jack, changing the subject.

'You can be so exasperating!'

'I know.'

Sophie shook her head. 'Incorrigible rascal,' she mumbled.

'Did you say something?'

'No. Let's order.'

It was getting dark and cooling down rapidly outside, the extreme desert climate showing its true colours. Goran and Markovich sat near the mine entrance, having a beer.

'He isn't coming,' said Goran and handed Markovich another can of beer.

'Looks that way,' Markovich admitted reluctantly. He hated being wrong. 'Let's go next door one more time and lean on the boys. Who knows what we'll find when we rattle their cage a little, eh?'

'All right. Let's do that.'

'You go ahead; I won't be long,' said Markovich and stood up.

Mitic turned to Ivanovich standing next to him. 'When he comes out next time, we move,' he said.

Ivanovich nodded. 'It's him, there's no doubt about it. He hasn't changed much since I interviewed him in the police station in Kosovo almost twenty years ago. Same aura of evil. Same imposing, intimidating man—'

'Who killed two guards with his bare hands, and then disappeared without a trace?' said Mitic.

'Until now. Here he comes!'

Mitic gave the agreed signal by raising his right hand. Three others waiting in the deserted street outside the mine – all seasoned veterans of the Kosovo war – raised their hands in silent reply.

Ivanovich looked at Mitic, nodded, reached under his shirt, pulled out a gun and crossed the street.

'Hello, *Slobodan*,' said Ivanovich as he walked up to Goran from behind. 'Fancy meeting you here after all these years.'

Goran was about to react when Ivanovich pressed the barrel of his gun against his back.

'In case you're wondering, it's a Glock, and the three guys walking behind me each have one too. So, don't do anything silly.'

'My name isn't Slobodan, it's Goran. What do you want?'

'Names are easy to change. Changing the past is a little more difficult. I want to continue our interview, which was so abruptly interrupted when you killed two guards, and then absconded. That may have happened a long time ago, but I don't think the facts have changed much, do you?'

'I don't know what you are talking about. This is stupid!'

'We'll see. Keep walking.'

'Where are we going?'

'To church.'

'I don't feel like praying.'

'Ah. By the time we're finished with you, you will; promise. Move!'

When Markovich came out of the mine and saw Goran walking down the deserted street surrounded by four men, he knew at once something was wrong. His military training told him that he was witnessing a professional abduction in progress. Instinctively, he stepped into the shadows, reached for the gun stuck in his belt, and then slowly followed the group down the street.

The trial in the rock church

Carved out of the sandstone by volunteers in 1992, the Serbian Orthodox Church of Saint Elijah the Prophet was unique. Because of the extreme Coober Pedy climate, where temperatures could reach more than forty degrees Celsius, the imposing church complex was located some seventeen metres below ground level at its lowest point. It consisted not only of a stunning church, with bass reliefs and stained-glass ceiling windows, but also housed a community hall, a priest's home and even a school. Little wonder it had become one of Coober Pedy's main drawcards.

The priest, also a former KLA fighter, met them at the entrance. 'Take him into the church,' he said. 'God will watch over this.'

Mitic nodded and led the way into the church. The priest locked the doors behind him and followed. It had been agreed earlier that a military-style hearing and trial would be conducted, with the priest presiding.

'The accused should stand in front of the altar and face us,' said the priest.

Ivanovich marched Goran down the aisle to the altar. It looked like he was leading a reluctant groom to a wedding he didn't want. 'Stand over there,' he commanded and pointed with his gun towards the altar.

'This is absurd,' said Goran, but did as he was told.

'Now, who will identify the accused and bring the accusations?' asked the priest.

Ivanovich stepped forward. 'I will,' he said, and then began to outline a catalogue of horrific war crimes Goran had been accused of in Kosovo just after the end of the Kosovo war in 1999.

Markovich had seen Goran and his minders enter the church. Used to making split-second decisions under pressure, Markovich considered what to do next. Obviously, he had to somehow get into the church to find out what was going on inside, and why. To him, the abduction, which had obviously been well planned, didn't make sense. Did it have something to do with his drug business, or the Desert Raiders, or was it somehow connected to the Drover's Retreat mine, Jimmy, and the opal? he wondered. In any event, he was determined to find out.

Slowly, Markovich walked along the front of the church until he found what he was looking for: some kind of side entrance. He tried the door. It was locked. While he didn't have tools of any kind with him, he did know how to improvise. Having picked many a lock in his time, Markovich knew exactly what to do. All he needed was a piece of wire, and he found it in the clasp of his Greek *komboloi* worry beads he always carried with him. It took him only moments to fashion the right tool, pick the simple lock and open the door.

Once inside, Markovich tried to orientate himself in the semi-darkness, the only light coming from a skylight in the ceiling. *Some kind of meeting room*, he thought, looking around the empty space full of stacked chairs facing a podium. Then he heard it: voices coming from a partially open door at the back of the room. As he made his way towards the door, he could clearly make out what was being said next door:

'... Rape, torture, random executions of dozens of civilians, including women and children, many hunted down in their homes, were all part of the crimes this man standing right here before God, was accused of,' Markovich could hear a man say. Once he reached the door – a side entrance leading into the church – Markovich could see Goran, hands tied behind his back, standing at the altar. The man speaking was pointing to Goran and addressing a group of men facing the altar.

The priest listened in silence until Ivanovich had finished. Then he turned towards Goran. 'What do you have to say about all this?' he asked, to give the improvised hearing at least some semblance of fairness, knowing full well the men in front of him had most likely already made up their minds.

'This is absurd! My name is Goran Petrovich. I've never been to Kosovo. This is all a big mistake,' said Goran, a defiant look on his face. 'I live in Alice Springs and work in a pub, the Drover's Retreat. The things you're accusing me of happened more than twenty years ago, for Christ's sake. On the other side of the world. You've got the wrong man!'

The priest looked at the men standing in front of him. 'You heard what the man said. Can any of you offer some credible evidence that links this man standing here before God to the atrocities you have just accused him of? In short, can you offer some *proof* that Goran Petrovich is in fact Slobodan Lazarevic, the Butcher of Pristina?' asked the priest. 'Because if you can't, you will be committing an injustice and a serious crime no different, morally speaking, from the ones you've just accused him of. So, think very carefully about this before we go any further. And please remember, we are standing in a house of God.'

After a long silence, Milan, who had earlier accidentally bumped into Goran in the street, stepped forward. 'There is someone who can,' he said softly. 'My wife, Radmilla. If I can persuade her to come here and face this monster, and more importantly perhaps, face a horrendous past too painful to remember, but impossible to forget,' added Milan.

'And she could identify this man and provide proof?' asked the priest.

'Yes, I believe she can. You have to hear what she has to say!'

'Then, please ask her to come here.'

Milan pulled his mobile out of his pocket. 'I'll call her,' he said. He walked over to the baptismal font in the side gallery and made a call. He returned moments later. 'She's on her way; she won't be long. As you know, we live close by. Our son is coming with her.'

'What now?' asked Goran, his tone defiant.

'We wait,' said the priest.

'This is a joke!'

'If that's so, you have nothing to worry about. In any case, we'll find out soon enough,' said the priest, and walked outside with Milan to unlock the church door.

Ten minutes later, the priest returned, followed by Milan leading his wife by the hand. His eighteen-year-old son, Marko, had his arm around his mother, who appeared frightened and distressed. As soon as she set eyes on Goran standing at the altar, she cried out and covered her face with her hands.

The priest waited for a few minutes to give Radmilla, a very religious woman, time to compose herself before asking the all-important question: 'Have you seen this man before?' he asked. 'Take a good look, and please remember that God is watching.'

'Yes, I have,' said Radmilla, shaking, her voice barely audible.

'Are you sure?' said the priest.

'Yes, absolutely.' Radmilla pointed to her head. 'Images of this man and what he did are etched into my brain like a burning memory, impossible to extinguish or forget.'

The priest nodded. 'Can you tell us about those memories?'

'Yes. Those memories are the reason I agreed to come here, because I want my son to witness this, and hear what happened. My husband, Milan, here already knows, because he was there and saw it all, but we have never discussed this with our son. He must know what happened to his grandparents and face the past, however painful and distressing.'

The priest pointed to Goran. 'And this is relevant to what we are trying to establish here; namely, this man's identity and past?'

'Yes, it is.'

'Then, please tell us.'

Taking a deep breath, Radmilla pointed to Goran. 'Slobodan Lazarevic, the man standing here before us, was known as the Butcher of Pristina for a very good reason. Not only for raping and killing innocent civilians, but for something much worse and diabolical. He was the right-hand man of Dritan Shehu – Doctor Death, as he was known in Kosovo at the time.'

Radmilla paused to compose herself, as painful memories came flooding back with alarming clarity and threatened to overwhelm her. 'Lazarevic and Shehu used the war as cover for a monstrous business they had set up in Kosovo, near the Albanian border, during the war.'

'What kind of business?' asked the priest, looking puzzled.

Radmilla took her time before answering, trying desperately to find the right words to describe the horror. 'Trafficking in body parts harvested from innocent civilians,' she whispered at last. 'Targeted and killed specifically for that purpose, a purpose that had nothing to do with the war—'

'Listen to her!' interrupted Goran. 'Now I'm being accused of—'

'*Silence!*' shouted the priest, pointing to Goran. 'You will speak when I give you permission. Interrupt once more and I'll gag you myself.'

Then turning towards Radmilla, the priest asked softly, 'How do you know this to be true?'

'Because of what I saw with my own eyes,' said Radmilla, tears streaming down her wan face.

Marko reached into his pocket, pulled out a handkerchief and handed it to his mother as a long moment of silence followed.

'Can you tell us more?' coaxed the priest.

Radmilla sighed. 'It was a Sunday in July 1998, a few days after my mother's birthday. It was very hot, and my parents and my sister were sitting outside having dinner when … they came to our farm.'

'Who came?' said the priest.

Radmilla pointed to Goran. 'That man over there, and four others. They arrived in some kind of military truck. They all had guns …'

'What happened?'

Radmilla turned to her husband standing next to her. 'I can't,' she stammered. 'You tell them.'

Milan nodded and looked up to face the priest. 'Radmilla was my girlfriend. We were both seventeen at the time. Our remote farms were next to each other, and we had grown up together.'

Milan paused, collecting his thoughts.

'On that particular night, we had dinner with my parents and were walking back to Radmilla's farm,' he continued, 'when we heard screams. It was already dark by then, and we ran towards the house to see what was happening. That's when we saw it …'

'Saw what?' asked the priest, bracing himself.

'Radmilla's father was kneeling on the ground. A man was pointing a gun at his head. Radmilla's mother and sister were lying on the dinner table being raped by two men. The men were all drinking, and there were empty bottles everywhere—' said Milan.

The priest held up his hand. '*Enough!* We get the picture. Where were you?'

'Hiding in the bushes nearby, watching,' said Milan.

'What happened next?'

Radmilla let out a scream and covered her face with her hands, trying in vain to banish the horror she had witnessed on that hot summer night.

'After the men had finished, they shot her mother and daughter in the back of the head. Moments later, they shot Radmilla's father, who had been made to watch,' said Milan, barely able to speak. 'Then they wrapped the corpses in blankets, threw them on the back of the truck and drove away.'

'Horrendous as all this must have been,' said the priest, 'how do we know this man here was actually there and participated in these atrocities? *Where is the proof?*'

Slowly, Radmilla turned to face Goran. She even took a step forward to get a little closer to him and raised her arm. 'The proof is on his back,' she said, her voice sounding confident and strong.

'What do you mean?' asked the priest, nonplussed.

'Because it was so hot that night, several of the men, including this one here, had taken off their shirts. While this man was raping my sister, he had his huge back to me. That's when I saw it – *clearly*.'

'Saw what?'

'A large tattoo.'

There was stunned silence as the implications of what Radmilla had just said began to sink in.

'I can see it right now, because it was so frightening,' continued Radmilla.

'Can you describe it?' said the priest.

'Yes. It was a large, grinning skull tattooed between his sweaty, hairy shoulder blades, with the letters UCK in red ink above, which stands for *Ushtria Clirimtare e Kosoves*.'

The priest nodded and walked over to Goran. 'Turn around!' he said.

Goran turned around.

Holding his breath, the priest began to slowly lift Goran's crumpled shirt.

Everyone in the church came closer for a better look, the silence leaden. The moment of reckoning had arrived.

First, the mandible appeared, then the teeth and the maxilla, followed by the zygomatic arch and the nasal bone, until the detailed outline of a complete human skull, wearing a red beret with the letters UCK above, stared accusingly back at them.

'What do you say now, Slobodan?' said the priest.

'Go to hell!' hissed Goran.

'Hell is where *you* are heading. Very soon, I'd say,' said the priest and turned to Radmilla watching him. 'We are done here. Thank you for being so courageous. Justice often comes at a very high price, but it's always worth it in the end. Marko, please take your mother home; leave the rest to us.'

After Marko and his mother had left the church, Ivanovich stepped forward and pointed to Goran. 'I have something to add that is relevant here because it throws further light on the atrocities committed by this man. It deals with the harvesting of body parts Radmilla mentioned earlier, in which this man here was implicated. I didn't want to talk about this before because it would have been too distressing for her. And especially for her son.'

'Go ahead,' said the priest.

'I was a young policeman in Burrel, a town near the Albanian border, when all of this happened. The atrocities just described by Milan and his wife were reported the next day, and I was sent to the farm to investigate. What had happened at the farm was by no means an isolated case. Similar incidents had been reported before and had one, curious thing in common: the bodies of those killed had all been taken away. Why? To conceal the crime? Hardly. The shocking answer came two days later. A local postman called us about something he had found at an abandoned farm nearby.'

Ivanovich paused, obviously upset as he remembered what he had discovered on that abandoned farm all those years ago.

'What was it?' prompted the priest.

'We found twelve bodies in a shed. All had gunshot wounds to the head and one more thing ...'

'What?' asked the priest.

'Their chests had been opened and their hearts surgically removed. And their kidneys as well. Can you imagine ...?' added Ivanovich quietly.

'Radmilla's parents and sister were among the bodies. We had heard rumours about an organ-trafficking racket operating in the area for months, but now we had proof. That's when we began our investigation and collected evidence that later resulted in a war crimes trial and the arrest of this man here and several of his accomplices. Shehu, Doctor Death, had gone to ground earlier and disappeared. We suspected he had left Kosovo on one of the small private planes used to transport the body parts to Istanbul, where they were sold on the lucrative black market, and then taken to the Middle East, to improve the lives of those rich enough to be able to afford a transplant. No questions asked.'

Ivanovich paused and looked thoughtfully at Goran's huge tattooed back, which had just provided a credible link between the man standing in front of him, and the man he had arrested all those years ago.

'I personally questioned Lazarevic after his arrest,' continued Ivanovich, 'but he managed to escape during the night after killing two of the guards, and vanished without a trace. Shehu surfaced years later as a highly respected surgeon, running a clinic specialising in transplants in Malta. He had changed his name to Fabry. Apparently, someone got to him before he could be exposed and prosecuted. He met a sticky end.'

'Did you know that, Slobodan?' asked the priest. 'The passage of time alone doesn't guarantee safety, as you are about to find out.'

Goran turned around slowly and smiled, his stance defiant.

'Very well,' said the priest and looked at the men watching him intently. They were all waiting for the next, final step.

'Now, the verdict,' said the priest. 'Are you satisfied that the man standing here before us is Slobodan Lazarevic, the man who has committed all those horrific crimes we have been told about?'

'We are,' came the unanimous reply.

'Then take him away. You know what to do. Evil such as this has no place in the eyes of God and must be erased!'

Markovich, who had quietly left the building after the verdict, understood what was happening. While Markovich had been in the army, he had not been involved in the organ-trafficking racket he had just heard about. He had inadvertently learned a lot about Goran he hadn't known before. To have a man with a past like that working for him was not only dangerous, but also reckless. It was definitely time to distance himself from Goran and get out of Coober Pedy.

Standing outside in the shadows, Markovich watched as Goran, surrounded by several men, was marched out of the church. With the priest leading the way, the strange procession had all the hallmarks of a walk to the gallows.

Curiosity getting the better of him, Markovich followed the group down the deserted street to a mine close by, until he saw them all walk inside and disappear, except for one man, who remained at the entrance to stand guard.

The execution

Jack and Sophie were having dinner on *The Ghan*, enjoying some quiet time after a hectic day full of frustrations and disappointments.

'How did you go with the concert arrangements?' said Jack. He reached across the table and refilled Sophie's glass.

'Benjamin has offered to step in and conduct. All considering, this is a good solution and should work well. He's an outstanding conductor. Very charismatic. I'm sure the audience will love him. And don't forget, we've included *Mat' Rossiya*, Tchaikovsky's lost symphony, in the program—'

'Which Benjamin conducted in the Bolshoi Zal in Saint Petersburg in 2017,' said Jack.

'Correct. Of course; you were there. Must have been quite something,' said Sophie, a tinge of envy in her voice. 'A world premiere of a recently discovered lost masterpiece by one of Russia's greatest composers.'

'It was unforgettable.'

'I can imagine.'

'And everyone understood your situation? About being stuck out here, I mean?' said Jack.

Sophie shrugged in resignation. 'Yes, I suppose so. I have an excellent team around me. They know how to deal with the unexpected, but still ...'

'Disappointed?' said Jack and put his hand on Sophie's arm.

'Yes, I am. Music is my life, and I was really looking forward to Adelaide, especially Tchaikovsky's lost symphony with Benjamin performing the violin solo.'

'I understand, but there's still time, you know.'

'Come on, Jack. You're a hopeless optimist! Have you heard from Andrew?'

'Not yet.'

'See? The concert's tomorrow and we are still stuck here in the desert, hundreds of kilometres away.'

107

'Hope has wings,' said Jack softly.

Sophie looked at Jack, her eyes glistening with emotion. 'Please don't misunderstand. I've had a wonderful time, Jack, and I appreciate everything you've done today, trying to keep me safe and get us to Adelaide, but it's time to admit defeat, don't you think?'

'Never! Shall we order some dessert? Strawberries look good.'

'And a hopeless romantic as well,' said Sophie, shaking her head.

When Jack turned around looking for the waitress, he saw Uncle Josh coming towards him from the other end of the dining car. 'Coming to join us?' said Jack.

'If you don't mind.'

'Certainly not; pull up a chair.'

'Better make that two.'

'How come?'

'Because there's someone else who would like to join you.'

'Oh? Who?'

'Ah, here he comes now,' said Uncle Josh.

'*Andrew?*' said Jack. 'I don't believe it!' He almost turned his chair over as he stood up and embraced his friend. 'How on earth did you get here?'

'Hope has wings, remember?' said Simpson.

Jack looked at Sophie. 'What did I tell you?' he said, beaming.

'Hello, Sophie. Enjoying the trip?' said Simpson and sat down. 'I hear you had a few unexpected adventures along the way ...'

Momentarily speechless, Sophie just looked at him, surprised, the colour green blurring her vision.

* * *

No-one said a word as the four men surrounding Goran followed the priest down into a long-abandoned mine shaft, the silence ominous.

'Can someone tell me where we are going?' asked Goran, trudging along with his hands tied behind his back.

'Where someone like you should feel right at home.'

108

'And where might that be?'

'The entrance to hell,' jeered Ivanovich. 'Where you belong.'

'Here we are,' said the priest. 'The end of the line, in more ways than one.' He pointed with his torch to a rock face blocking the way. 'This is a good spot to bury evil.'

Milan, an experienced miner, put down his backpack and looked around. 'Over there,' he said. 'I'll set the charge right here in the ceiling. That should do it.'

'Good idea,' said one of the men standing next to Goran. 'It will bring it down.'

'Bring what down?' asked Goran, aware he didn't have long to live.

'The ceiling; what else?' said the priest. 'Hog-tie him, boys.'

'With pleasure,' said Ivanovich and began to expertly tie Goran's hands and feet together, making him totally immobile.

Resigned to his fate, Goran didn't resist, but the arrogance in his demeanour remained. 'Make it quick,' he growled.

'You'll go out with a bang,' said Milan, pushing a stick of dynamite into a crevice, 'when *we* decide ...'

* * *

'I don't believe this,' said Sophie, watching Simpson. 'You have a plane?'

'Yes. A Cessna 172 Skyhawk named *Nelly*. I've had her for thirty years. Still going strong. Most successful small aircraft ever built. Jack here knows all about it; don't you, mate?'

'Sure do,' said Jack, enjoying his second brandy after dinner. 'We flew around the Kimberley in this plane, looking for Anna. What an adventure that was! Andrew's one hell of a pilot, I tell you.'

'Landing at Kalumburu, the remote Benedictine Mission, and then at Never Never Downs Station during a storm, remember?' reminisced Simpson.

'Without Andrew and his plane, we wouldn't have found Anna,' said Jack. 'How long did it take you to get here?'

'Just under four hours. The weather was good and the wind kind.'

Jack nodded. 'How long to Adelaide, do you think?'

'About the same time, all going well. We should leave at first light. That should give our celebrity conductor here enough time to get some beauty sleep before preparing for the concert. What do you reckon, mate?'

'Fine by me,' said Jack. 'Another brandy?'

'Why not?' said Simpson.

Sophie held up her hand. 'Okay, guys. Do I understand you correctly: we are flying to Adelaide in *Nelly* first thing tomorrow morning?'

'Yep, that's it,' said Jack. 'Better pack your stuff tonight.'

Sophie shook her head. 'I better call my team and tell them about this.'

'Good idea. And could you please arrange a ticket for Andrew? He would love to come to the concert; wouldn't you, mate?'

'Absolutely. Wouldn't miss it for quids! And by the way, Rusty says hello. He was wondering if we could perhaps put on a concert in the Outback sometime. After a race, perhaps? He reckons Rosie and Olive would love it,' said Simpson, a sparkle in his eyes. 'Especially the percussion section.'

Jack turned to Sophie and handed her another brandy. 'Hope has wings, see? I told you so. Cheers.'

'Incorrigible rascals,' mumbled Sophie, gritting her teeth. 'Both of you!'

After Jack and Sophie had excused themselves and returned to their cabin, Uncle Josh and Simpson – both tribal elders and *kurdaitcha* men – climbed off *The Ghan* and walked slowly into the night.

Step by step, they left the train and modern life behind, and entered a different realm: the ancient spirit world of their ancestors.

'What do you think happened to Jimmy?' asked Simpson.

'I think Toby's telling the truth. Markovich and the Moloch killed him and somehow disposed of the body. The police searched the train but found nothing. No trace of Jimmy, nor Markovich or the Moloch. I think they lost interest. Hardly surprising.'

'What about the opal?'

'Jimmy had it with him. He showed it to me. I've never seen anything like it. An extraordinary find.'

'Do you know what happened to it?'

'No.'

'Do you think the Desert Raiders got their hands on it?'

'I doubt it. The opal is in control here, not men.'

'The curse?' said Simpson.

'Yes. Opals fight evil and destroy those who covet them for the wrong reasons.'

Uncle Josh picked up a few dry branches and began to build a small fire.

'Very well. Let's see what we can find out about all this,' said Simpson. 'Are you ready?'

'Yes, I am,' said Uncle Josh and began to chant. He looked up at the stars – home of his ancestors – and asked for permission to enter the spirit world.

Simpson pulled two *bilma* – clapsticks – out of his pocket and began to tap the sticks together to maintain rhythm during the chant while Uncle Josh fell into a trance, and slowly began to dance around the fire.

* * *

'Ready,' said Milan. He'd adjusted the detonator and set the timer.

The priest walked over to Goran lying on the floor, hands and feet awkwardly tied together. He looked like some strange beast about to be sacrificed on a pagan altar. 'Do you have anything to say before you meet your maker?' asked the priest.

Goran turned his head slowly and looked at the priest with contempt. 'We both know there is no God. So why don't you fuck off and get on with whatever you're doing, and let's get this over with!'

'Very well. May God have mercy on your soul,' said the priest and turned away. 'All right, guys, let's go, and leave this monster to his fate.'

As the men walked away and the mine shaft descended once again into darkness, Goran began to laugh. An evil, bone-chilling laugh of a condemned man about to die a horrible death, which none of the other men who heard it would ever forget.

Once back outside in the open, Milan took a deep breath to calm himself and looked at his watch. 'About now,' he said. Moments later, a loud explosion rocked the old mine shaft as the dynamite ripped the ancient sandstone walls apart, causing the ceiling to collapse. Crushed to a pulp by the enormous weight of the rocks, Goran had joined the realm of precious opals and ancient fossils, his dark soul trapped underground to do penance for sins too monstrous to warrant forgiveness.

Standing close by in the shadows, Markovich had been watching the mine entrance. He had heard the thud, felt the tremor, and had seen the jubilant men walk out of the mine without Goran. Fully aware of what must have happened, and why, he realised it was time to get out of Coober Pedy as quickly as possible.

* * *

The spirit of Jandamarra had witnessed it all. Satisfied the opal curse had done its work, the spirit drifted out of the collapsed mine shaft and across the sleeping desert towards Uncle Josh, dancing slowly around the fire.

Uncle Josh felt the spirit approach and began to tremble as images of a body lying next to railway tracks began to take shape in his mind's eye. Then Jandamarra materialised, floated down to the body and pointed to the bloody head.

'Jimmy!' mumbled Uncle Josh as he recognised the face. 'Now I know what happened to you, and where you are.'

The concert in Adelaide: Saturday 28 May

Nelly took off just after sunrise. Coober Pedy looked very different from above, the white mounds of excavated debris, which reminded Jack of molehills, the only evidence of the vast network of underground mine shafts that criss-crossed the sandstone like endless tunnels of hope.

Jack sat next to Simpson in the front of the plane, and Sophie just behind him.

'There, look, the church,' said Jack, pointing down. 'It's hard to believe what's below that hill, carved out of solid rock by volunteers. *By hand!*'

'Amazing,' said Sophie, in awe. 'And there, look, *The Ghan.*'

The long train with its polished steel carriages glistening in the morning sun looked like a giant silver snake sunning itself in the desert while greeting a new day.

'To make the journey a little more interesting, we'll fly over Wilpena Pound and the Flinders Ranges. One of the most stunning sights in South Australia, especially from above,' said Simpson as the plane began to climb. 'Especially on a day like this. The colours will be amazing.'

'What's Wilpena Pound?' Sophie asked.

'Wait till you see it,' said Jack. 'It looks like a giant meteor crater, but it isn't. It's a natural land formation; an amphitheatre-like ring of mountains in the heart of the Flinders Ranges National Park. Extraordinary!'

'According to Aboriginal Dreamtime stories handed down through the ages, Wilpena Pound was created by two giant serpents who devoured an entire tribe – men, women and children – who had gathered for celebrations. Unable to move after the huge meal, the head of the male serpent became Saint Mary's Peak, and the female's head became Beatrice Hill. We'll be flying over both of them.'

'This is wonderful,' said Sophie.

'Hans Heysen, one of Australia's best known landscape painters, found his inspiration for his famous watercolours of majestic

Australian gum trees in the Flinders Ranges,' said Jack. 'I walked part of the Heysen trail, a spectacular long-distance walk through the Flinders Ranges, with Rusty and his mates a few years ago.'

'Incredible! It's hard to believe that, all going well, I could be conducting the South Australian Symphony Orchestra in Adelaide this evening,' said Sophie. 'It's almost surreal. Perhaps I, too, will get some inspiration from this ancient landscape that I can draw on.'

'I'm sure you will,' said Jack. 'There's no ill wind that doesn't blow some good, see? If that derailment accident hadn't stopped *The Ghan*, we wouldn't be up here to see all this.'

'True, Mister Optimist.'

'Hope has wings, remember?'

'All right, I give up. You win,' said Sophie, laughing.

'What did Benjamin say when you told him that you're going to make it after all?' said Jack.

'He wasn't surprised. Do you want to know why?'

'Tell me.'

'Because apparently you have friends who somehow always seem to get you out of tight corners. Isn't that right, Andrew?'

'How true,' said Simpson. 'That's Jack. We should be in Adelaide in about four hours.'

'Perfect. I will have to go straight to the Festival Centre for rehearsals, if that's okay.'

'No problem,' said Simpson. 'On one condition.'

'What's that?'

'I get a ticket for tonight's performance.'

'Already arranged. You're sitting next to Jack,' said Sophie, laughing.

'Do I have to?'

'Yes. Concert's fully booked.'

'Bummer!'

After a breathtaking flight over the Flinders Ranges and the famous Barossa Valley, Simpson touched down safely in Adelaide just before ten am.

'I can't tell you how much this means to me,' said Jack as Simpson opened the luggage locker behind the rear seats. 'To miss the concert would have been devastating for Sophie. And for me,' he added softly. 'I can't thank you enough.'

'You would have done the same,' said Simpson.

As he handed Jack his duffel bag, a strange feeling washed over Simpson, and he could hear Uncle Josh whisper in his ear: *Remember, the opal is in control, not men. The gemstone will show itself when the time is right.* Simpson looked thoughtfully at the bag in Jack's hand. It seemed to be telling him something.

'And besides, you seem to have mates who are always getting you out of trouble,' continued Simpson, shrugging off the strange sensation.

'Looks that way,' said Jack, smiling. 'You said you're staying with friends. I'll take Sophie straight to the Festival Centre for the rehearsals, if you don't mind. That concert should be really something.'

'Looking forward to it,' said Simpson. 'See you tonight. Make sure you have my ticket!'

'Will do. Meet you in the foyer for a glass of champagne?'

'Sounds great.'

As Simpson closed the luggage locker, Sophie walked over to him and gave him a peck on the cheek. 'Your blood's worth bottling,' she said. 'Thanks, Andrew!'

'Outback lingo; not bad. Jack taught you this?'

'He did. He also said he wouldn't have missed this for quids.'

'Did he now? I hope he didn't teach you some of his other favourite Aussie sayings ...'

'Like what?'

Simpson shook his head. 'Not fit for a lady about to conduct a symphony orchestra. More for the ear of a camel like Rosie about to start a race.'

'There's a difference?' said Sophie, laughing.

'I hope so!' replied Simpson, enjoying the banter. 'Off you go! Good luck with the rehearsal. See you both at the concert.'

After dropping Sophie off at the Festival Centre, Jack went straight to the Intercontinental, which was close by, and checked in.

Looking for some quiet time to reflect on the turbulent events of the past week, Jack took a long walk along the banks of the River Torrens near the hotel, and then strolled through the Botanic Gardens, to clear his head.

Strange, he thought, how the threads of the past were catching up with him, not only through people he knew well, like Krakowski, Gonski, Carrington and Dr Rosen, but also through music, especially Sophie and her unique talent.

First, there was Krakowski's violin concerto performed by the maestro himself in Sydney on his famous violin, the Empress, and now *Mat' Rossiya*, Tchaikovsky's lost symphony, was reaching out of the past in a dramatic way, reminding him of his adventures in Russia, which had almost cost him his life.

And then, of course, there was the enigmatic Uncle Josh; someone who had known Gurrul, whom Jack had been very close to since childhood. Another strange coincidence? Or was it? Jack asked himself as he remembered the Dreamtime stories Gurrul had told him over many a campfire in the Outback, and the Dreamtime stories told by Uncle Josh on *The Ghan* just the other day.

As he walked back to the hotel, Jack wondered what had happened to the precious opal that seemed to have started it all. It couldn't have just vanished without a trace. Then he recalled what Uncle Josh had said about the curse of the opal: 'The opal is in control here, not men.' *I wonder* ... thought Jack, and went to his room to take a shower and prepare for the evening.

Sophie, Krakowski, and their entourage were staying in the same hotel, but on a different floor. Carrington and Gonski had flown in from Sydney earlier that day and were also staying at the Intercontinental.

Because clothes were not his forte, Jack always travelled light. The shirt and dress pants he had brought along especially for the concert definitely needed ironing. Jack set up the ironing board, took the shirt out of his duffel bag and ironed it. After hanging up the shirt, he remembered the cufflinks and began to look for them.

The well-travelled duffel bag had many pockets and various compartments, inside and out. When Jack opened one of the side pockets he rarely used, and reached inside hoping to find his cufflinks, he found something unexpected that made the hairs on the back of his neck tingle.

Jack was waiting for Simpson in the busy foyer of the Festival Centre, as arranged. Simpson was late, and Jack was about to go to his seat when Simpson walked in. 'Sorry, mate,' said Simpson, looking flustered. 'Taxi was hard to get.'

'Don't worry. Here's your ticket,' said Jack. 'Let's go inside. Performance is about to start. You're in for a treat, my friend.'

'Can't wait!'

Thunderous applause erupted as soon as Sophie entered and joined the orchestra on stage. After taking a deep bow, she waited until the enthusiastic welcome had ebbed away. Then she turned towards Krakowski sitting next to the First Violin behind her.

'Ladies and gentlemen, before we begin, Maestro Krakowski, who, as most of you would know, conducted the world premiere of Tchaikovsky's lost symphony in Saint Petersburg not that long ago, would like to say a few words. Maestro ... please ...' said Sophie and stepped away from the microphone.

'Thank you,' said Krakowski and stood up. 'Ladies and gentlemen, what you're about to hear is not only a masterpiece by one of Russia's greatest composers, but it's also a piece of history. As your programmes would have told you, this symphony was only recently discovered, and how that happened is a remarkable story in itself, which is now inextricably linked to this extraordinary work.

'I was privileged to have been invited to conduct the premiere of this masterpiece in the Bolshoi Zal in Saint Petersburg in 2017, but what is not generally known is that just before the concert, Tchaikovsky's original score with his handwritten notations was presented to the Governor of Saint Petersburg at the composer's grave in the Tikhvin Cemetery, where all the great Russian composers are buried. It was a brief and moving ceremony, which was only possible because the cemetery was in the centre of Saint Petersburg, not far from the concert venue.

'The reason I'm telling you all this, ladies and gentlemen, is because the man who was instrumental in discovering *Mat' Rossiya*, Tchaikovsky's lost symphony, and who returned it to Russia at the composer's gravesite just before the premiere, is right here tonight.'

Krakowski, an experienced public speaker, paused to let the tension grow and kept looking at Jack sitting in one of the rows directly in front of him.

'The man I'm talking about is Jack Rogan, celebrated author and dear friend, who, in his bestselling novel, *The Lost Symphony*, has written about the extraordinary journey of this masterpiece, how it was discovered, and how it was finally returned to where it belongs: to Russia, the composer's homeland. Jack, would you please stand up.'

Taken aback and a little embarrassed, Jack stood up and took a bow as applause erupted all around him.

'Now, without further ado, let Tchaikovsky's genius transport you into the world of *Mat' Rossiya*, the lost symphony.'

With that, Krakowski returned to his seat. Sophie turned around to face the orchestra and lifted her baton, the sudden hush in the concert hall electric.

'You're a famous bastard,' whispered Simpson as Jack sat down. Jack poked him in the ribs with his elbow in silent reply, as the first stirring notes of Tchaikovsky's masterpiece filled the concert hall with sublime sound.

'That was incredible,' said Simpson after the final curtain call. 'I have never heard anything like it. Sophie was amazing, and so was your friend – the violin virtuoso with the funny name. What an ending to an exciting day. Coober Pedy in the morning, and now this.'

'It's not over yet,' said Jack as they made their way to the exit.

'What do you mean?'

'I've arranged supper at the Intercontinental just around the corner, and, of course, you're invited. Everyone will be there: Sophie, Benjamin, and a few of my friends from Sydney I want you to meet. It's close by. We can walk.'

Simpson shook his head. 'You're certainly a different man in the big smoke.'

'And that's not all. I have a big surprise for you. I can hardly believe it myself, but there it is.'

'What kind of surprise?'

'Destiny has shown its hand ...'

'I don't understand. What hand?'

'You'll see ... soon. Let's go back to the hotel. I could kill for a cold beer. What about you?'

'Now you're talking. At least I can understand that bit.'

Yurlunggur

Jack had booked a private dining room at the Intercontinental for an intimate post-concert supper. Krakowski and Dr Rosen arrived first, and were joined by Sophie, Carrington and Gonski a short time later. Everyone was on a high after the spectacular success of the concert.

Encouraged by the standing ovation and shouts of 'More! More!', Krakowski had played a breathtaking encore – Paganini's *Caprice No.24 in A Minor* – which brought the house down and resulted in almost endless curtain calls.

Jack walked over to Krakowski and embraced him. 'That was truly something, Benjamin,' he said. 'Let me introduce you to a good friend of mine: Andrew Simpson.'

'Ah, the man who came to Sophie's rescue with his plane,' said Krakowski. 'Pleased to meet you. Without your help, we wouldn't have had a concert quite like this; isn't that right, Sophie?'

'Who knows? But it would have been different, for sure. I owe Andrew a lot.'

Simpson shrugged and waved dismissively. 'It was spectacular! Your violin solo—'

'Paganini never disappoints,' said Krakowski.

'Neither does Benjamin. It was one of his father's favourite pieces,' said Dr Rosen. 'He was a child prodigy, known throughout Europe.'

'That's true. This was the piece he played for Count Esterhazy after the count presented him with the famous violin during a concert in Vienna in 1905 that almost didn't go ahead,' said Krakowski.

'Because his own violin had been stolen by gypsies the night before,' said Jack, stepping in.

'Correct.' Krakowski pointed to the violin case on the chair behind him. 'That's how the Empress became a Krakowski family treasure. My father was only fourteen at the time.'

'May I see it?' said Simpson.

'Sure.' Krakowski opened the violin case, took out the Empress and held it up. 'A genuine Stradivarius with an extraordinary history. It

120

was named after Kaiser Franz Joseph's wife, Elizabeth – the Kaiserin, the Empress – in 1867. Hence the name.'

'Magnificent,' said Simpson.

Jack turned to Krakowski and pointed to the violin. 'Do you think it was this Paganini piece your father played for Monet in his garden in 1920? With this very violin?'

'When Monet presented him with *Little Sparrow in the Garden*, you mean?' said Carrington, who knew the story well. 'The painting that caused so much controversy?'

'The Fuchs affair, with the forgery?' interjected Gonski.

'Could be. As I said, it was one of his favourite pieces because it showed off his virtuosity to perfection,' said Krakowski.

'Just as it has done tonight,' said Jack. 'Must be in the genes. This calls for a toast.' Jack signalled to the drink waiter and pointed to an ice bucket with several bottles of Veuve Clicquot ready to be opened.

During the splendid meal everyone began to relax, assisted by copious quantities of French champagne.

'When are you going to tell us about your outback adventure, Jack?' asked Dr Rosen, well aware it wouldn't take much to get the storyteller in Jack going.

'Now, if you like,' said Jack, who had been waiting for just such an opening. He put his serviette on the table and reached for his glass. 'It's difficult to believe so much can happen in a week; isn't that right, Sophie?'

'Sure is.'

'Tell us about it,' prompted Carrington.

Jack took a sip of champagne, sat back in his chair, and then described the events of the past week with his usual eloquence and storytelling flair he was so well known for. He began with the camel race in Alice Springs and had his friends in stitches when he talked about Rusty and Rosie, and the rowdy night at the Drover's Retreat after the race had been lost because a stray dog had run across the racetrack. He showed them photos on his iPhone of Olive the python wrapped around Sophie's neck and shoulders, and then introduced the subject of the opal find in Coober Pedy, and Simpson's request to investigate the circumstances of the opal's extraordinary discovery.

After that, the subject became more serious, as Jack spoke about the notorious Desert Raiders and their part in the opal saga. He also mentioned Uncle Josh, his Aboriginal Dreamtime stories and the warning about the opal curse.

Leaving nothing out, Jack told his enthralled audience what had happened during the night *The Ghan* returned to Manguri after a freight train derailment had blocked the track, and described the frightening encounter with Markovich and the Moloch in the crowded cabin. Finally, he spoke about Toby, and what he had told them about Jimmy's murder he claimed to have witnessed in the kitchen on the train ...

'Priceless opals, murder and ruthless villains? This sounds more like an *Indiana Jones* movie than a trip on a luxury train,' said Dr Rosen, shaking her head. 'No doubt about you, Jack, you are definitely an adventure magnet. I don't know how these adventures find you all the time.'

'It's all about his breadcrumbs of destiny,' said Gonski. 'He just follows them, and there you have it.'

'You can say that again,' said Sophie, softly. 'It happened just like Jack said. Looking back, it's a miracle we made it here to Adelaide in time for the concert. And that was only possible because of you, Andrew.'

'You rewarded me with an unforgettable performance,' said Simpson, a sparkle in his eyes.

'A small reward for a big favour,' said Sophie.

Carrington, who knew Jack well, had been following Jack's account of what had happened with interest. Having heard many of Jack's stories over the years, he realised the narrative was building up to some kind of climax, which was classic Jack, who liked to surprise his audience with the unexpected.

'Something bothers me,' said Carrington, an experienced trial lawyer, used to spotting flaws in a case.

'What's that?' asked Jack.

'What happened to the opal? Do you know?'

'Ah. I'm glad you asked,' said Jack, grateful for the cue. 'The reason I'm telling you all this in such detail, is because of something that happened just a few hours ago. Right here, in my hotel room. It was a bolt out of the blue I am still having difficulty coming to terms with.'

Jack paused and looked around the table, to let the tension grow.

'Tell us,' said Carrington.

'It's all about this,' said Jack. Slowly, like a magician introducing his next trick, he reached into his jacket pocket, pulled out something wrapped in what looked like a large handkerchief, and placed it carefully on the table in front of him.

'What is it, Jack?' asked Sophie, craning her neck.

Jack pointed to the small bundle in front of him. 'Why don't you have a look?'

'All right,' said Sophie. She stood up, walked over to Jack, leaned over and began to unfold the handkerchief. Moments later, she withdrew her hands as if pricked by a hot needle, and gasped.

'Is that what I think it is?' said Simpson after a while, breaking the stunned silence.

'It is. This is *Yurlunggur*, the spectacular opal found by Jimmy Bingarra in the Coober Pedy mine a few days ago. This is the precious gemstone that seems to have been the reason for his murder,' said Jack.

'How on earth did you get it?' asked Simpson, his voice hoarse with surprise.

'This afternoon, when I opened one of the side pockets of my duffel bag that I rarely use, it was in there.'

'Just like that?' said Simpson.

'Yes.'

'How do you think it got there?' asked Carrington.

Jack shrugged. 'No idea. The only logical explanation is that Jimmy must have somehow hidden it there ...'

'Well, this entire matter is full of mysteries,' said Simpson. 'I may as well throw another one in the ring.'

'What do you mean?' asked Jack.

'As you know, I spent last night with the boys at our mine in Coober Pedy. I also spoke with Uncle Josh just before we left this morning.'

'And?' prompted Jack.

'Rumours were circulating through the tight-knit Coober Pedy community.'

'What kind of rumours?'

'Rumours about a ritual execution.'

'*What?*' said Carrington. 'This is becoming more bizarre by the minute.'

'Perhaps, but that's Coober Pedy,' said Simpson. 'Especially as far as the Serbian miners are concerned. It's a harsh place, full of secrets.'

'What kind of rumour?'

'Apparently, there was a trial of a Kosovo war criminal in the Serbian Orthodox church last night, followed by an execution in one of the mines operated by the Serbs.'

'Are you serious?' asked Carrington, looking stunned.

'Yes.'

'What kind of execution?' asked Jack.

'The convicted man was buried alive in one of the abandoned mine shafts. Apparently, dynamite was used.'

'How awful,' said Sophie.

Jack, who sensed where this was heading, asked the next question.

'How is this relevant? Do we know who the convicted man was?'

'Yes. It was the Moloch. The Desert Raider's enforcer who was on *The Ghan.*'

'What about Markovich, the other one?'

'Disappeared without a trace,' said Simpson. 'According to Uncle Josh, who was not in the least surprised, all this has to do with the opal fighting evil.'

'I need a drink,' said Gonski, shaking her head.

'Good idea,' said Jack and reached for a champagne bottle in the ice bucket. 'All I can say is that opal mining is a dangerous business.'

'And so is travelling with you, Jack,' said Sophie.

'Touché!' said Jack, smiling. 'Another drink, anyone?'

Sophie sat up in bed and looked at Jack, packing his duffel bag. 'You're up early. What time is it?'

'Almost time for me to go. I'm flying back to Alice with Andrew, remember?'

'Of course. You told me.'

'That was some concert last night. You must be very proud.'

'It did go well. The South Australian Symphony Orchestra was a pleasure to conduct, but Benjamin was definitely the star. He had the audience in the palm of his hand.'

'He couldn't have done it without you.'

'I suppose not. We're a good team.'

'You certainly are. So, Melbourne's next?'

'Yes. The next concert's the day after tomorrow. Our flight's at lunchtime today. Rehearsals start tomorrow morning. After that, we're off to New Zealand.'

'You're a globetrotting celebrity.' Jack sat down on the edge of the bed and reached for Sophie's hand. He realised it was time to return to their respective lives. Reality had overtaken the fairytale.

'I hate goodbyes,' he said.

'So do I.'

'So, why don't we just say *auf Wiedersehen?*'

'Good idea. You're going back to Alice; why?'

'Loose ends. I promised Andrew to help him with the sale of the opal. It's worth a fortune and it belongs to his rehabilitation centre. The money will go a long way, if invested wisely.'

'So, this is it, then?'

'Yes.' Jack bent down and kissed Sophie tenderly on the forehead. 'Keep following your star, whatever fancy colour it may be.'

'And you just follow those breadcrumbs of destiny everyone keeps talking about. Who knows? One day they may lead you to ...'

Sophie didn't complete the sentence, but turned away, tears welling. Once again, her career was demanding its pound of flesh: lonely nights in exchange for the magic of music.

Jack stood up, reached for his duffel bag and walked to the door. Just before he reached it, Sophie wiped away a few tears and looked at Jack, standing at the door.

'I wouldn't have missed this for quids,' she said softly.

'Neither would I,' replied Jack, and then quickly left the room.

Alice Springs: one week later

It took three days before things returned to normal on the busy Adelaide-to-Darwin line. Because of the remote location of the accident, moving the derailed freight train and repairing the damaged tracks had turned out to be more difficult and time consuming than originally thought, causing chaos in the meantime.

As one of the freight trains from Darwin came through and slowly approached the newly restored section of the tracks, the train driver noticed something that looked like a body lying in the mulga scrub and reported what he had seen to authorities.

Police from Coober Pedy were sent to investigate and did find a body. It turned out to be Jimmy.

When Uncle Josh heard the news, he wasn't surprised. It all supported Toby's account of what had happened during that fateful night on *The Ghan*. However, what was at odds with Toby's testimony was the finding by the police that the injuries sustained by Jimmy were consistent with a fall or jump from a moving train, and had nothing to do with murder. After that, the authorities quickly lost interest and closed the case.

Pursuing another more complex and delicate line of enquiry, which could have involved the notorious Desert Raiders and implicated them in a murder, didn't seem warranted. This was especially so because a convicted Aboriginal youth on parole, a stowaway without any family ties, was involved. The body was released and a routine report prepared for the coroner. It would take months before that report reached the courts. By then, all would have been long forgotten.

The authorities may have abandoned Jimmy and discarded another possible interpretation of what could have happened to him, but not Uncle Josh. To him, the fact the opal had made a surprise appearance and ended up in the right hands was an important sign.

Another telling sign that the opal's power was in play was the Moloch's surprise execution. That only left Markovich at large, and Uncle Josh was determined that he too would pay for Jimmy's murder and not go unpunished. Tribal law demanded that.

127

It was well after midnight when Uncle Josh walked down the deserted street in front of the Drover's Retreat. The patrons had left a long time ago and all was quiet. Almost directly opposite the pub was an empty block of land frequented by stray dogs and the occasional drunk sleeping off a long night on the booze after closing time.

For Uncle Josh, however, this was the perfect place for what he had in mind. As a *kurdaitcha* man, he was permitted by tribal law to perform the ancient Aboriginal execution ritual of pointing the bone, used since time immemorial to punish the guilty by willing death.

Wearing traditional oval shoes known as *intathurta*, woven of emu feathers and human hair soaked in blood, Uncle Josh was ready. Hidden in a sacred place in the desert, these all-important ceremonial shoes had once belonged to his father, also a *kurdaitcha* man. They were only used for ritual purposes and played a crucial role in bone pointing.

Another important ritual object was the *kundela*, the killing bone fashioned out of a kangaroo's tibia. About fifteen centimetres in length, it looked like a long needle with a strand of hair threaded through a hole in the bone at the rounded end. Uncle Josh had earlier charged the *kundela* with lethal psychic powers directed at Markovich, who was asleep in his bedroom on the first floor of the pub, directly opposite the block of land.

Slowly, Uncle Josh put on a mask made of emu feathers that identified him as a ritual executioner, and began to recite the ancient curse known as the *kurdaitcha* chant. Then he went down on one knee and pointed the *kundela*, the killing bone, at Markovich's bedroom while at the same time imagining Markovich lying in his bed.

Markovich was now a condemned man and Uncle Josh was certain that death would follow soon. Content that the ritual had been performed as tradition demanded, Uncle Josh returned to his car parked at the end of the street and drove out into the desert.

Once the lights of Alice had been left behind, Uncle Josh stopped the car, got out, and built a small fire. Remembering his ancestors, he looked up at the stars, and then threw the *kundela* into the fire for the ritual burning.

As the *kundela* began to burn, a fire broke out on the first floor of the Drover's Retreat and quickly spread to Markovich's bedroom. By the time the fire brigade arrived, the entire first floor of the pub was well alight and the heat so intense that getting inside the building was impossible.

It took the firefighters several hours to extinguish the flames. By then, the veranda had collapsed and the roof had caved in. Markovich's incinerated body was found under sheets of corrugated iron from the roof, which covered the charred remains like a steely shroud.

News of the fire and Markovich's death raced through Alice the next morning and half the population came to have a look at the ruins, which were still smouldering. Jack, who was due to fly back to Sydney later that day, did the same. As he looked at what was left of the historic pub, rather than see the end of an era like most of the spectators around him, he saw an opportunity.

Drover's Retreat: one year later

It was almost dark by the time Jack got out of the taxi and looked at the imposing structure, oozing outback character and charm. It had been a long flight from Paris, but he was very much looking forward to the opening.

Wow! he thought, well pleased with what he saw. First impressions were always important. Until then, he had only seen plans for the reconstruction of the iconic building, largely destroyed by the fire a year earlier.

Doors look the same, he concluded as he walked towards the crowded entrance full of eager patrons trying to get in. The noise coming from inside was deafening.

'You made it, after all,' said a voice coming from behind just as Jack was about to walk through the swinging doors.

Jack spun around. 'Andrew! Place looks fantastic!' Jack dropped his duffel bag and embraced his friend. 'I don't know how you did it. Getting the place ready for the opening day we planned months ago, I mean.'

'Wasn't easy. We worked round the clock for weeks and had a lot of help. Guys came from far and near to lend a hand. Changing the date was unthinkable. The race is tomorrow, remember? Camel Cup!'

'Of course. Still ...'

'Come inside and let me show you round.'

'I've been up since dawn and it's been an exhausting flight. Had to change planes in Sydney. I came straight from the airport. I could kill for a beer,' said Jack.

'No problem. We've got plenty of that!'

Inside, the atmosphere was electric. Not only was it incredibly loud and crowded, but it was also difficult to believe that so many people could fit into a confined space. The hum of excited voices almost drowned out the band playing country and western music in the courtyard.

As Jack followed Simpson to the bar, he remembered what the smouldering ruins of the Drover's Retreat had looked like the morning after the pub had burned down. A lot had happened since then, and it was difficult to imagine how the iconic establishment had managed to rise out of the ashes to begin a new chapter in its long, albeit turbulent history.

First, Jack had helped Simpson to organise the sale of the priceless opal. Choosing the right auction house and preparing a clever advertising campaign to give the rare gemstone international exposure had made a huge difference, not only to the spirited bidding at the auction, but ultimately the result.

Jack had turned to his friend Isis, retired mega-rockstar turned art collector and philanthropist, for help at the time, and it was only through Isis's contacts that a major London auction house agreed to become involved and took on the unique antipodean project.

During the lead-up to the auction, *Yurlunggur*, the stunning Coober Pedy opal from Down Under, became a celebrity, and even featured in TV commercials promoting Coober Pedy as one of the most unique mining towns on the planet and a must-see tourist destination.

Due mainly to this unprecedented and slick advertising campaign arranged by the auction house, the London auction was a huge success. Surpassing all expectations, the unique opal sold for just over two million pounds to an anonymous collector from Oman.

Suddenly, Simpson's modest Aboriginal youth rehabilitation project financed entirely by donations and operated by volunteers, had some serious money. The challenge that remained was what to do with it, and how to put the extraordinary opportunity to good use.

Once again, Jack had stepped in to help. He showed Simpson how to set up an appropriate structure: a foundation to help young Aboriginal offenders to integrate into the community, and find employment and accommodation after doing prison time. After all, Jack reminded himself, the mining claim in Coober Pedy, which had been instrumental in finding the precious gemstone in the first place, had been set up for precisely that purpose. It was therefore logical to focus the new foundation's activities on similar rehabilitation projects.

'Jack, before I show you round, I want to say something.' Simpson put his hand on Jack's arm and looked at him intently.

'In hindsight, to buy the Drover's Retreat – what was left of it – with the opal money was a masterstroke. Everyone thought we were crazy at the time – me included – remember? I'm sure they're no longer saying that when they see this.'

'You're right; it was a bit of a leap of faith,' said Jack, smiling. 'But here we are. A bit ironic too, don't you think?'

'Young Aboriginal offenders just out of jail, running the Drover's Retreat once owned by the notorious and much-feared Desert Raiders, you mean?'

'There's a little more to it. Strict supervision and realistic parole conditions, but yes, exactly,' said Jack. 'This has a much better chance of providing integration than alcohol bans and impossible bail conditions.'

'I've been saying this for years, but nobody listened,' said Simpson.

'Until now. You are leading by example.'

'Thanks to you, mate.'

Jack waved dismissively. 'Now, what about that beer you promised?'

'Coming up.'

'Dining room looks great, and so does the bar. I love the decor. Very original,' said Jack while waiting for his beer at the main bar.

'Rusty came up with all this. You wouldn't think so, but he's actually very artistic, with a lot of imagination. We wanted to give the place an authentic outback feel, and what better way to do this than using unique and original artefacts, like those wonderful old drover's saddles above the bar, complete with bridles, whips and old boots? Or that wooden propeller from an early biplane, a Tiger Moth, or the pair of wheels over there that once belonged to a Cobb & Co stagecoach?'

Simpson pointed to the ceiling above the bar. 'And there, look, that's a radiator and headlights from a 1910 Model T Ford, would you believe?'

'Now I've seen everything. Impressive!'

'There's more. Wait till you see the courtyard! We have an original Southern Cross windmill that used to pump water for almost a hundred years out there. Rusty found it on one of the cattle stations not far from here. The stuff he scavenged is absolutely amazing! The tourists love this! Just look around you. We're onto something special here, I tell you.'

'I can see that.'

'Rusty came up with the names, as well. We called the dining room 'Jimmy's Grill' – you can guess why – and over there we have the Snake Bar, Olive's favourite spot, and next to it is Storyteller's Corner.'

'What's that all about?'

'That's Uncle Josh's spot. After dinner, guests can listen to Dreamtime stories.'

'You're kidding!'

'No. Tourists love it, especially the ladies. And so do the locals; trust me. Uncle Josh has given *The Ghan* away, and is now doing this.'

'Impressive.'

'Nothing like having a few cold beers and listening to Uncle Josh. As you know, he's a master storyteller. Just like someone else I know,' said Simpson and slapped Jack on the back. 'Come, there's a spot over there at the Snake Bar,' said Simpson and began to push through the crowd.

'So, the official opening's tomorrow, after the race?' said Jack, kicking his duffel bag under the barstool.

'Yes. The icing on the cake would be if Rosie wins the race and the Larapinta Cup comes here. Rusty would bring Rosie straight back here, as the cup winner. He's built a pen for her in the courtyard.'

'You are joking, surely?' said Jack, looking incredulous.

'No, I'll show you. He's our manager, you know. Doing a fabulous job, I can tell you, and he brings Rosie to work occasionally. He lives on the premises upstairs. She's very social. Loves people. So far, she's been a great hit.'

Jack downed his beer and slammed the empty glass on the bar, smacking his lips.

'Another?' asked Simpson.

'You bet. All these success stories have made me thirsty.'

'Coming up. How many pubs do you know that have a racing camel in the courtyard next to an open grill, and a Ford Model T radiator complete with headlights hanging above the bar?'

'I don't know what to say. You're full of surprises, mate.'

'Speaking of surprises, the best is yet to come,' said Simpson, sounding conspiratorial, 'as someone I know well keeps telling me.'

'What do you mean?'

'Patience. I'll be right back in a jiffy. Watch my seat.'

'Will do,' said Jack and reached for his beer.

'Is that seat free?' asked someone softly.

'Sorry, luv,' said Jack, 'it's taken.'

'Pity, I would love to have had a chat about breadcrumbs and destiny.'

Jack looked over his shoulder and gasped, his eyes wide with disbelief. '*You? Here?* It can't be!'

'But it is,' said Sophie and sat on the barstool next to Jack. 'Are you going to buy this sheila a drink, or what?'

Simpsons Gap: the next day

After having spent an eventful evening at the Drover's Retreat with Rusty, Simpson and Uncle Josh – and even Olive making an appearance – Jack and Sophie went back to Simpson's Wandjina Gallery in the early hours of the morning.

The next day was all about the race that the whole of Alice was talking about. The Larapinta Cup had become famous, drawing crowds from far and near. The main race was due to start at noon. Preliminary races were at ten am, with Rosie the favourite to win the cup.

'The Drover's Retreat even has a beer tent this year,' said Simpson, serving breakfast for his house guests. 'Better get there early; the crowds will be something else. There isn't a spare bed in Alice and many people are sleeping in their cars. I think the whole of the Northern Territory has come here for the race.'

'I hope Rosie wins this time,' said Sophie, enjoying her hearty bacon and eggs after a long night drinking with the boys.

'Rusty will be very disappointed if she doesn't. As long as he manages to stay in the saddle, all should go well,' said Simpson, smiling as he remembered the dog fiasco and Rusty's spectacular fall in last year's race.

'What you've done with the place is astonishing,' said Jack. 'Last night was extraordinary. What a crowd and what an atmosphere. Outback Oz at its best.'

'I agree,' said Sophie. 'Thanks again for inviting me.'

'Pleasure. So, what's the plan for today, guys?'

'We'll go straight to the races from here,' said Jack, 'and then go with the flow. Sophie has to fly back to Japan tomorrow. Concert in Osaka.'

'Good plan,' said Simpson. 'More toast, anyone?'

'Why not?' said Jack and pushed his plate across the table. 'And a few more mushrooms, if I may.'

'What is it with you, Jack? You and food. Always starving,' said Sophie.

'You know me too well. Thanks, Andrew. This is going to be quite a day.'

Jack and Sophie arrived at the racetrack just before eleven.

'Just look at this crowd,' said Jack, working his way towards the Drover's Retreat beer tent. As he came closer, he ran into several of his mates from the night before.

'Do you think any of these guys have gone home to have a sleep?' said Sophie.

'Judging by the way they look, I doubt it. A few sore heads here, for sure.' Jack pointed to the makeshift bar in the tent. 'Look who's over there,' he said.

'Isn't that Toby from *The Ghan*?'

'It is. Andrew's given him a job. He's working in the pub. One of the many success stories. First, the boys go and work in the mine. If they behave and obey the rules, they're given a job at the pub and learn about hospitality. If that works out, they get a reference and, hopefully, find employment in the community. That's the plan.'

'That's wonderful.'

'It is. I think Andrew and the Dinkarra Foundation, as it's called, have hit on something here that actually works. Andrew just bought a vacant block of land for the Foundation, directly opposite the Drover's Retreat. Do you know what for?'

'Tell me.'

'To build a microbrewery.'

'What? Brew their own beer?'

'Exactly. And serve it at the pub under their own label: Drover's Lager; Drover's Pale Ale; Drover's Pilsener ...'

'That's brilliant!'

'It is. And behind the brewery, they're planning to build a hostel for the staff. Somewhere for the guys on the program to live. I strongly supported that.'

'You never told me what happened to the Desert Raiders,' said Sophie.

'As you know, Markovich, the president of the outlaw motorcycle club, died in that fire. That was the beginning of the end of the Desert Raiders, which in essence was a criminal enterprise controlling the drug business in the Outback. Without Markovich's leadership, the whole organisation fell apart. A liquidator was appointed – by the tax department, I believe – and the building was put up for sale. Andrew saw an opportunity and bought the property.'

'Andrew said it was your idea.'

'It may have been.'

'You're a man of many colours, Jack, that's for sure.'

'Just like the music you can see, in colour? What was that fancy term now?'

'Synaesthesia.'

'That's it. I wonder, what colour am I?'

'That depends.'

'On what?'

'That's a secret.'

'You're teasing me.'

'Perhaps just a little.'

'The race is about to start. I better go and place a few bets …'

'You're going to see the man with the large leather bag over there, right?'

'Yes, the bookie. He's a mate. Bound to give me good odds. Stay right here. Don't go anywhere!'

Jack returned a few minutes later and found a good spot in front of the beer tent for them to watch the race. Moments later, the tinny loudspeakers crackled into life and announced the race everyone had been waiting for. The much-anticipated Larapinta Cup was about to start.

In many ways, the race mirrored last year's, except for the stray dog. Rosie got off to a good start and led all the way. As she approached the final turn, Rambo was closing in from behind in the inside lane, but Rusty saw him coming. Leaning forward, Rusty kept talking to Rosie and told her to put on more speed, which she did and, to the delight of the roaring crowd, Rosie and Rusty won the race.

By the time Jack returned to the tent after collecting his winnings – a tidy sum – celebrations in the beer tent had already started. 'This calls for a drink,' he said excitedly.

'I guess so,' said Sophie, rolling her eyes.

When Rusty appeared holding up the Larapinta Cup, which would go on display in the pub behind the Snake Bar, celebrations began in earnest.

'Jack, may I have a word?' said Sophie, after Rusty had given her a bear hug that lifted her off her feet.

'Sure. What is it?'

'Would you mind very much if we were to leave? Right now, I mean?'

Jack looked at Sophie, surprised. 'Are you feeling unwell?'

'No. Quite the opposite, in fact.'

'I don't understand.'

'I'm flying back to Japan tomorrow morning.'

'I know.'

'I'd like to spend some quiet time with you before I leave,' said Sophie softly.

'Sure. I'm sorry; I know this is all a bit rough and tumble.'

'It's not that. It's just that time's very precious. And I've come a long way ...'

'You sure have.'

'To see *you.*'

Silence.

'Was that the reason you came?'

'Of course it was. Andrew arranged it all. At my request. As a surprise for you.'

'I know you and Benjamin made large donations to the foundation. I thought that was why—?'

'Nonsense! You can be exasperatingly naïve, Jack!'

'Ah,' said Jack, feeling quite foolish and embarrassed. 'I'm sorry, it's just that I—'

Sophie put a finger on Jack's lips. 'There's no need to say anything, Jack. Let's go somewhere quiet. I have a place in mind.'

'You have?'

'Yes. You took me there once before. Every time I think about our trip last year, I see that place. Something about it affected me deeply. I think it was the colours at sunset.'

'What place?'

'Simpsons Gap. Nothing to do with Andrew, as you explained at the time.'

'That's right. It's named after A. Simpson, President of the Royal Geographical Society of South Australia. The Simpson Desert is also named in his honour,' said Jack. 'A spiritual place full of ancient dreaming stories.'

'Yes. It was incredibly beautiful, and every time I remember it, I can hear music and see the colour red. The red of those ancient, soaring cliffs on both sides of the waterhole.'

'It's only a short drive from here. We could be there in half an hour.'

'Would you mind?'

Jack reached for Sophie's hand. 'Not at all, but there's one condition.'

'What condition?'

'As a man of many colours, I have to know what colour I am. In your eyes, I mean. You must tell me. I'm too afraid to ask about the music,' said Jack, a sparkle in his eyes.

'I'll think about it.'

'All right. Let's go.'

'It's just as beautiful as I remember it,' said Sophie as they walked into the gorge cut by Roe Creek through the West MacDonnell Ranges. Sophie sat down on a rock and looked up at the red cliffs towering above her. 'There's something about this place. Something spiritual that touches your soul.'

'There are many places like that in the Outback. I've come across a number of them, especially in the Kimberley. Gurrul, my childhood mentor and friend, showed me some of these places and explained their meaning. What makes them so special is their connection to Aboriginal Dreamtime stories and countless generations past. This place is a good example. The Arrernte people call it *Rungutjirpa*.'

'It's so peaceful here, so serene. Are there Dreamtime stories that specifically belong here?'

'There are. In fact, several dreaming trails intersect here at this spiritual site.' Jack pointed to a giant ghost gum rising out of the sandy soil next to a rare permanent waterhole. 'Just imagine: Aboriginal elders sitting under that tree, telling spellbound youngsters that *Rungutjirpa* was the mythological home of giant goanna ancestors who once roamed the earth.'

Sophie reached for Jack's hand. 'I'll tell you why I wanted to come here,' she said quietly. 'When I look back, our whirlwind outback trip last year was like a Wagnerian opera. It had it all. Heroes and villains, good fighting evil, a priceless gemstone, danger, exotic settings, and a brutal murder, all rubbing shoulders with ancient Aboriginal Dreamtime stories about an opal curse, retribution and justice.'

'You're right. It was an unforgettable week, in more ways than one.'

'Quite so and in a way, the reopening of the Drover's Retreat is the final chapter of that extraordinary story, don't you think?'

'Yes, you could say that.'

'Yet, there was so much more.'

'Oh, yes? What?'

Sophie took her time before replying.

'*Love*,' she said softly, her eyes shining with emotion. 'The most precious gem of all. That's why I wanted to come here with you. Because for some reason I can't explain, it's this place I see every time I think about ... *you*.' Sophie paused, collecting her thoughts. 'And when I do, I *ache*.'

'Is that why you came? To tell me this?' said Jack, his voice quivering with emotion.

'Yes, and to give you a present.'

'A present? What kind of present?'

Sophie reached into her shoulder bag, pulled out an envelope and handed it to Jack.

'What's this?'

'Open it.'

Jack opened the envelope and looked inside. 'Is that what I think it is? An airline ticket?'

'Yes. To Osaka. Same flight as mine. Departing tomorrow night from Sydney.'

Taken aback, Jack looked at Sophie.

'I have a few free days after the concert before I fly to Vancouver to continue the tour. Last year, you showed me some of your favourite places here in the Outback. I would like to show you one of mine in Japan: Kyoto. It's only an hour by fast train from Osaka.'

'You want me to come with you to Japan? Tomorrow?'

'Yes, but if for whatever reason you can't, I understand,' whispered Sophie, the apprehension in her voice palpable because she had just bared her soul and felt vulnerable. 'What do you say?'

For a while, Jack stared wistfully at the ancient ghost gum near the waterhole, aware he was looking at a fork in the road, and not just the gnarled branches of a mighty tree.

Slowly, Jack turned to face Sophie. 'I wouldn't miss it for quids,' he said, a cheeky grin spreading across his face.

'In that case, I'll tell you.'

'Tell me what?'

'It's blue,' said Sophie, smiling, as relief and happiness washed over her.

'What is?'

'The colour of *you*.'

'Makes sense, I suppose,' said Jack.

'Why do you say that?'

'Because blue's the colour of hope.'

'So?'

'Isn't it obvious?'

'Is it? Why?'

'Because incorrigible rascals always live in hope, don't they?'

More Books by the Author

The Empress Holds the Key (Jack Rogan Mysteries Book 1)
The Disappearance of Anna Popov (Jack Rogan Mysteries Book 2)
The Hidden Genes of Professor K (Jack Rogan Mysteries Book 3)
Professor K: The Final Quest (Jack Rogan Mysteries Book 4)
The Curious Case of the Missing Head (Jack Rogan Mysteries Book 5)
The Lost Symphony (Jack Rogan Mysteries Book 6)
The Death Mask Murders (Jack Rogan Mysteries Book 7)
The Stolen Altarpiece (Jack Rogan Mysteries Book 8)

In 2013, I released my first adventure thriller –
The Empress Holds the Key.

THE EMPRESS HOLDS THE KEY

A disturbing, edge-of-your-seat historical mystery thriller

Jack Rogan Mysteries Book 1

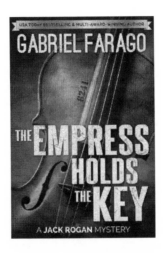

Dark secrets. A holy relic. An ancient quest reignited.

Jack Rogan's discovery of a disturbing old photograph in the ashes of a rural Australian cottage draws the journalist into a dangerous hunt with the ultimate stakes.

The tangled web of clues – including hoards of Nazi gold, hidden Swiss bank accounts, and a long-forgotten mass grave – implicate wealthy banker Sir Eric Newman and lead to a trial with shocking revelations.

A holy relic mysteriously erased from the pages of history is suddenly up for grabs to those willing to sacrifice everything to find it. Rogan and his companions must follow historical leads through ancient Egypt, to the Crusades and the Knights Templar, to uncover a secret that could destroy the foundations of the Catholic Church and challenge the history of Christianity itself.

Will Rogan succeed in bringing the dark mystery into the light, or will the powers desperately working against him ensure the ancient truths remain buried forever?

The Empress Holds the Key
is now available in ebook and paperback

Encouraged by the reception of *The Empress Holds the Key*, I released
my next thriller – *The Disappearance of Anna Popov* – in 2014.

THE DISAPPEARANCE OF ANNA POPOV

A dark, page-turning psychological thriller

Jack Rogan Mysteries Book 2

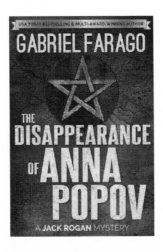

**A mysterious disappearance. An outlaw bikie gang. One dangerous
A mysterious disappearance. An outlaw bikie gang. One
dangerous investigation.**

Journalist Jack Rogan cannot resist a good mystery. When he stumbles
across a hidden clue about the tragic disappearance of two girls from
Alice Springs years earlier, he's determined to investigate.

Joining forces with his New York literary agent; a retired
Aboriginal police officer; and Cassandra, an enigmatic psychic, Rogan
enters the dark and dangerous world of an outlaw bikie gang ruled by
an evil master.

Entangled in a web of violence, superstition and fear, Rogan and
his friends follow the trail of the missing girls into the remote
Dreamtime-wilderness of Outback Australia, where they face their
greatest challenge yet.

Cassandra has a secret agenda of her own and uses her occult powers to conjure up an epic showdown where the stakes are high, and the loser faces death and oblivion.

Will Rogan succeed in finding the truth, or will the forces of evil prevail, causing untold misery and destroying even more lives?

Gold Medal Winner in Psychological Mysteries
– Thriller Category
The Global Book Awards 2022

The Disappearance of Anna Popov
is now available in ebook and paperback

My next book, *The Hidden Genes of Professor K*, was released in 2016.

THE HIDDEN GENES OF PROFESSOR K

A dark, disturbing and nail-biting medical thriller

Jack Rogan Mysteries Book 3

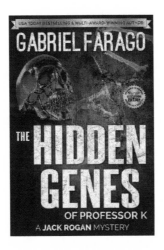

A medical breakthrough. A greedy pharmaceutical magnate. A brutal double-murder. One tangled web of lies.

World-renowned scientist Professor K is close to a groundbreaking discovery. He's also dying. With his last breath, he anoints Dr Alexandra Delacroix as his successor and pleads with her to carry on his work.

But powerful forces will stop at nothing to possess the research, unwittingly plunging Delacroix into a treacherous world of unbridled ambition and greed.

Desperate and alone, she turns to celebrated author and journalist Jack Rogan.

Rogan must help Delacroix, while also assisting famous rock star Isis in the seemingly unrelated investigation into the brutal murder of her parents.

With the support of Isis's resourceful PA, Lola; a former police officer; a tireless campaigner for the destitute and forgotten; and a gifted boy with psychic powers, Rogan exposes a complex web of fiercely guarded secrets and heinous crimes of the past that can ruin them all and change history.

Will the dreams of a visionary scientist with the power to change the future of medicine fall into the wrong hands, or will his genius benefit mankind and prevent untold misery and suffering for generations to come?

"Outstanding Thriller" of 2017
Independent Author Network Book of the Year Awards

The Hidden Genes of Professor K
is now available in ebook and paperback

My next book, *Professor K: The Final Quest*,
was released in October 2018.

PROFESSOR K: THE FINAL QUEST

An action-packed historical medical mystery

Jack Rogan Mysteries Book 4

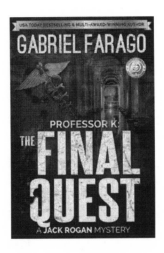

**A desperate plea from the Vatican. A kidnapped chef. An
ambitious mob boss. One perilous game.**

When Professor Alexandra Delacroix is called in to find a cure for the
dying pope, she follows clues left by her mentor and friend, the late
Professor K, which lead her on a breathtaking search through
historical secrets, some of them deadly.

Her old friend Jack Rogan must step in to assist while also
searching for kidnapped Top Chef Europe winner Lorenza da Baggio.

He joins forces with his young friend and gifted psychic, Tristan; a
dedicated Mafia-hunting prosecutor; a fearless young police officer;
and an enigmatic Egyptian detective who is on a perilous hunt for a
notorious IS terrorist.

Together, they stand off with the head of a powerful Mafia family in Florence and uncover a network of corruption and heinous crimes reaching to the very top.

Will Rogan and his friends succeed in finding Lorenza and curing the pope, or will the dark forces swirling around them prevail in their sinister plots?

Gold Medal Winner in the Fiction – Thriller – Medical Category
Readers' Favorite 2019 International Book Awards Contest

Professor K: The Final Quest
is now available ebook and paperback

My fifth book, *The Curious Case of the Missing Head*,
was released in November 2019.

THE CURIOUS CASE OF THE MISSING HEAD

A gripping medical thriller

Jack Rogan Mysteries Book 5

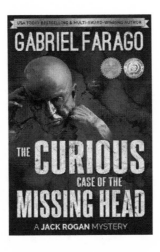

**A headless body on a boat. An international conspiracy. Can a
kidnapped genius survive a controversial scientific discovery?**
Esteemed Australian journalist Jack Rogan is on a mission to solve the
disappearance of his mother in the 1970s. But when a friend needs
help rescuing a kidnapped world-renowned astrophysicist, he doesn't
hesitate. Struggling with more questions than answers, his investigation
leads them aboard a hellish hospital ship, where instead of finding the
kidnap victim, he's confronted with a decapitated corpse.

As the search intensifies, Jack bumps up against diabolical cartels
with hidden agendas. And when his research reveals dubious
experiments, a criminal on death row, and a shocking revelation about
his mother's fate, he must uncover how it's all linked.

Can Jack unravel the twisted connections and catch the scientist's
killer, or will the next obituary published be his own?

Gold Medal Winner in the Fiction – Thriller
– Conspiracy Category
Readers' Favorite 2020 International Book Awards Contest

"Outstanding Thriller/Suspense" of 2020
Independent Author Network Book of the Year Awards

The Curious Case of the Missing Head
is now available ebook and paperback

My sixth book, *The Lost Symphony*, was released in November 2020.

THE LOST SYMPHONY

A historical mystery thriller

Jack Rogan Mysteries Book 6

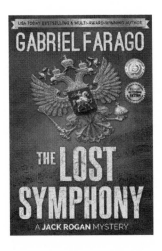

A murdered tsarina. A lost musical masterpiece. A stolen Russian icon. Can Jack honour a promise made a long time ago, and solve an age-old mystery?

When acclaimed Australian journalist and author Jack Rogan inherits an old music box with a curious letter hidden inside, he decides to investigate. As he delves deeper into a murky past of secrets and violence, he soon discovers he's not the only one interested in solving the puzzle.

Frieda Malenkova, a ruthless art dealer; and Victor Sokolov, a Russian billionaire with a dark past, will stop at nothing to achieve their dark desires and foil Jack's valiant struggle to uncover the truth.

Joining forces with Mademoiselle Darrieux, a flamboyant Paris socialite; and Claude Dupree, a retired French police officer, Jack enters a dangerous world of unbridled ambition, murder and greed that threatens to destroy him.

On a perilous journey that takes him deep into Russia, Jack follows a tortuous path of discovery, disappointment and betrayal that brings him face to face with his destiny.

Will Jack unravel the hidden clues left behind by a desperate empress? Can he save the precious legacy of a genius before it's too late, and return a holy icon revered by generations to where it belongs?

Gold Medal Winner in the Fiction – Mystery – Historical Category
Readers' Favorite 2021 International Book Awards Contest

Award-Winning Finalist in the Fiction: Thriller/ Adventure Category
The 2021 International Book Awards

"Outstanding Mystery" of 2021 - Mystery Category Winner
Independent Author Network Book of the Year Awards

The Lost Symphony
is now available in ebook and paperback

My seventh book, *The Death Mask Murders*,
was released in December 2021.

THE DEATH MASK MURDERS

A historical mystery crime thriller

Jack Rogan Mysteries Book 7

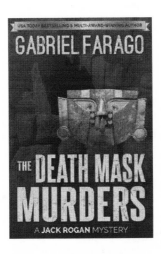

Seven brutal murders. A cursed Inca burial mask. A lost treasure. One deadly game.

When convicted killer Maurice Landru reaches out from a Paris prison and asks for help to prove his innocence, celebrated author Jack Rogan cannot resist. Drawn into a web of hidden clues pointing to an ancient mystery, Jack decides to investigate.

Joining forces with Francesca Bartolli, a glamorous criminal profiler; Mademoiselle Darrieux, an eccentric Paris socialite; and Claude Dupree, a retired French police officer, Jack enters a dangerous world of depraved cyber-gambling, where the stakes are high and the players will stop at nothing to satisfy their dark desires.

Following his 'breadcrumbs of destiny', Jack soon comes up against an evil genius who terminates his enemies without mercy and is prepared to risk all to win.

On a perilous journey littered with violence and death, Jack uncovers dark secrets of a murky past of ruthless conquistadors, bloodthirsty pirates and shipwrecked priests, all pointing to a fabulous treasure, waiting to be discovered.

Can Jack expose the mastermind behind the horrific murders and retrieve the legendary treasure before it falls into the wrong hands, or will the forces of darkness overwhelm him and destroy everything he believes in?

Gold Medal Winner in the Fiction – Mystery - Historical Category
Readers' Favorite 2022 International Book Awards Contest

"Outstanding Mystery" of 2022 - Mystery Category Winner
Independent Author Network Book of the Year Awards

The Death Mask Murders
is now available in ebook and paperback

My latest book, *The Stolen Altarpiece*, was released in April 2023.

THE STOLEN ALTARPIECE

A historical mystery crime thriller
Jack Rogan Mysteries Book 8

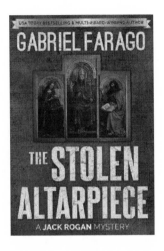

A long-forgotten amulet. A stolen painting. A dark threat reignited. One deadly geopolitical power-play.
Jack Rogan's discovery of a hidden letter reaching out of the past unwittingly embarks the journalist into a perilous quest to find a holy relic that has the power to fight evil.

As he follows a web of intriguing clues that take him on a dangerous journey to the Middle East, Rogan soon crosses swords with an old adversary, who is determined to destroy him and those he holds dear.

Soon, secrets buried in a famous stolen painting point to Russia and the threat of war in Ukraine. Joining forces with Tristan, a gifted psychic; Abbot Serapion, a Russian monk; and Sasha, the daughter of a Russian billionaire, Jack enters a dangerous geopolitical arena ruled by a deranged, corrupt man consumed by unbridled ambition and lust for power, who threatens to enslave a nation and destroy an entire country to satisfy his misguided vision of greatness.

Can Jack find a way to defeat the dark forces of evil and turn the tide of history before it's too late, or will the horrors of war continue, and consume a people who dared to stand against tyranny and dream of freedom?

Gold Medal Winner in the Fiction - Thriller - Political Category
Readers' Favorite 2023 International Book Awards Contest

Gold Medal Winner in Amateur Sleuth - Thriller Category
The Global Book Awards 2023

The Stolen Altarpiece
is now available in ebook and paperback

About the Author

Gabriel Farago is the *USA TODAY* best-selling and multi-award-winning Australian author of *The Jack Rogan Mysteries Series* for the thinking reader.

As a lawyer with a passion for history and archaeology, Gabriel Farago had to wait many years before being able to pursue another passion – writing – in earnest. However, his love of books and storytelling started long before that.

'I remember as a young boy reading biographies and history books with a torch under the bed covers,' he recalls, 'and then writing stories about archaeologists and explorers the next day, instead of doing homework. While I regularly got into trouble for this, I believe we can only do well in our endeavours if we are passionate about the things we love. For me, writing has become a passion.'

Born in Budapest, Gabriel grew up in postwar Europe and, after fleeing Hungary with his parents during the Revolution in 1956, he went to school in Austria before arriving in Australia as a teenager. This allowed him to become multilingual and feel 'at home' in different countries and diverse cultures.

Shaped by a long legal career and experiences spanning several decades and continents, his is a mature voice that speaks in many tongues. Gabriel holds degrees in literature and law, speaks several languages and takes research and authenticity very seriously. Inquisitive by nature, he studied Egyptology and learned to read the hieroglyphs. He travels extensively and visits all the locations mentioned in his books.

'I try to weave fact and fiction into a seamless storyline,' he explains. 'By blurring the boundaries between the two, the reader is never quite sure where one ends, and the other begins. This is, of course, quite deliberate, as it creates the illusion of authenticity and reality in a work that is pure fiction. A successful work of fiction is a balancing act: reality must rub shoulders with imagination in a way that is both entertaining and plausible.'

Gabriel lives just outside Sydney, Australia, in the Blue Mountains, surrounded by a World Heritage National Park. 'The beauty and solitude of this unique environment,' he points out, 'gives me the inspiration and energy to weave my thoughts and ideas into stories that in turn, I sincerely hope, will entertain and inspire my readers.'

Gabriel Farago

Author's Note

I hope you enjoyed reading this book as much as I enjoyed writing it. I'd be very grateful if you'd post a short review on Amazon. Your support really does make a difference.

CONNECT WITH THE AUTHOR

Amazon
https://www.amazon.com/stores/
Gabriel-Farago/author/B00GUVY2UW

Website
https://gabrielfarago.com.au/

Goodreads
https://www.goodreads.com/author/show/7435911.Gabriel_Farago

Facebook
https://www.facebook.com/GabrielFaragoAuthor

BookBub
https://www.bookbub.com/profile/gabriel-farago

Sign up for the author's New Releases mailing list and get a free copy of *The Forgotten Painting** novella, to find out where it all began ...

https://gabrielfarago.com.au/free-download-forgotten-painting/

* I'm delighted to tell you that *The Forgotten Painting* has just received two major literary awards in the US. It was awarded the Gold Medal by Readers' Favorite in the Short Stories and Novellas category and was named the 'Outstanding Novella' of 2018 by the Independent Author Network (IAN) Book of the Year Awards.

Made in the USA
Middletown, DE
15 January 2024

47911330R00106